JULIE CHAPPELL

Homecoming

and Other Mythic Tales

For Hank Jones and Michael Dooley,
and all the stories yet to be written
at the kitchen table and thereabouts.

Contents

Uncle Ollie's Legacy

Annie walked slowly around the corner of the dilapidated old house, sizing up its potential and not really watching her step. "Shit! Snake! Shit!" She did a Texas two-step around the coiled reptile lying just at the corner of the cracked stone steps leading up to the back porch of the house.

Timber rattler or harmless rat snake, she couldn't be sure so she jumped up the porch steps watching each foot as she went.

"Snakes, broken steps, cracked foundation, big ass spiders…all mine." She spoke as if to someone standing nearby, but the closest living thing to her was still the snake at the foot of the steps.

Well, hell, she thought, same snakes as where I grew up—rattlesnakes, copperheads, water moccasins. Grandma used to leave a saucer of milk for a blacksnake that lived in the basement of the old farmhouse. She claimed it kept him there eating all the mice and rats from the fields. Of course, snakes don't drink milk unless there's nothing else. But who would tell Grandma that? She lived fully in her myths and legends.

"Maybe I should move to Ireland. No snakes. Good beer. Friendly people. Myths and legends not connected to my family." Her words floated out and faded away as she turned to gaze beyond the steps to the top of The Mountain. That's what the locals called it anyway, The Mountain. She had lived near real mountain ranges in her life and visited plenty of others so was not impressed by this hill. But she freely admitted that the view of the flatland to the north and east were awe-inspiring.

"Is the view enough to sink money into this place, restore the old house, replant the plum and pear trees?" She wondered aloud. Talking to herself was a lifelong habit and never felt strange. She did worry that one day in the not-too-distant future she would be that old lady, mumbling to herself in the grocery store or on the sidewalk in town.

Annie continued into the house and wandered about inside until the heat and the adrenalin from the unexpected snake brought on a headache. She pulled a BC powder out of the stash in her purse and looked for her water bottle, finding it in the last of the four rooms in this poor house, the room she might eventually call hers if this place could ever be put to rights. The powder worked in the blink of an eye so the headache was quickly relieved while its 65mg of caffeine rejolted her system.

"Better get out of here before I pass out from all the excitement and heat. I'd probably wake up with that damned snake coiled around my head," she kept her voice low this time as she spoke to the empty air.

No lock on the decrepit front door so she didn't need to do anything to close up except to pull the front door to and push the concrete block against the back door screen to keep larger critters out of the house. That done, she climbed into her old, yellow International Scout, put the key in the ignition, took a breath, and held it until the engine caught.

"I hope someone around here knows how to work on you, old girl."

The Scout responded with only a bit of a sputter as Annie steered it down the washed out, sparsely graveled road traversing the edges of the land around the house that would lead eventually to the main road. As the car left the dirt and gravel, it lurched forward before gaining proper purchase on the asphalt road that wound around the back of The Mountain and onto the highway to town.

An image of a green chile cheeseburger with jalapeño slices started to form in Annie's head as she aimed her car at the little town nearby.

"Why, oh, why do you stick in my head, green chile burger and biting hot jalapeños! Well, maybe the restaurant is closed so I can't give in to your seductive ways!"

And closed it was, since most restaurants in the town only stayed open until about 3PM. Lunch only, except for the one or two chains on the far side of town. Turning around and heading for the larger small town about 30 miles west, Annie spotted an old rock house set back a bit off the road.

"Well, I'll be damned, The Edge of Town. A cafe? Bar? Derelict building?"

The sign on the door, one of those with two sides, *Open* or *Closed*, was still turned to the *Open* side. She pulled off the highway and bumped again onto another washed-out dirt and gravel drive. Only a couple of trucks were parked obliquely near the front door so she pulled in between them with just enough room on both sides for the drivers to get back into their trucks without denting her Scout. As she shut her engine off, Annie could see that the place was more a pile of stones with a screen door wedged into it than a "house," rock or otherwise.

"Oh, well, if it has food and drink. I'm good." She looked around suddenly aware that, this time, when she spoke out loud to herself, she might not be alone. She tossed her head slightly as if to shake something off, straightened her back, and walked through the screen door.

Hmm. The Edge of Town is certainly, well, edgy, she thought, as her eyes tried to adjust to the dimmer, darker inside. O.K. dim and drab, but…what's that smell? Oh, deep fried everything!

She breathed in the aromas as she headed for a table in the corner, then realized that the bartender was eyeing her as she crossed the room. Go to the bar, she reminded herself. You are not in the city anymore.

"Hi. Do you have a menu?"

"Sure. Here ya go. Do you want somethin' ta drink?"

"Please. Tecate? With lime? And salt?"

"Comin' up."

Annie put half a butt cheek on the closest stool and peered down at the one-sheet menu in her hand. Fried dill pickles. Chicken fried steak. Chicken fried chicken? Jalapeño poppers. Cheeseburger. The menu was a cornucopia of fried foods.

"I'll have an order of poppers and a cheeseburger, please." Annie shoved the money across the bar.

"Just take a seat, and I'll bring it out in a bit."

Annie took her beer and walked back across the floor to a table. Table's a bit wobbly, she judged, but gives a good view of the place. Check out the quirks of art! Old license plate, Longhorn skull, buffalo head with requisite dust and cobwebs—Animal skins of unknown species! Is that a bird or what? Just what I love about rural Texas. Homey, no pretentions. Peanut shells on the floor remind me of that place we used to go in Kansas City.

On the table next to her, a colored piece of paper with a blurry photo in the center caught her eye. Texas Jambalaya. Singer-songwriters Zack, Dan, and LoRena playin' your favorites.

Texas with a little Cajun underneath, she wondered? Or Cajun with a little Texas on the side? This place is livelier than the rest of the town. I might just stay.

Her food arrived in the hands of the bartender/waitress, and Annie dove in. She was hungry now, her headache receding with every bite.

My first rural Texas honky-tonk. Burger's good. And Texas Jambalaya for a mere $5.00 cover. But, will I look like a desperate woman if I stay to hear the band? Who cares? Each bite settled her discomfort as the place began to fill up.

The bartender set beer after beer on the bar as now a younger, but not swifter, waitress roamed among the tables. Then Annie noticed a very tall, old man with sunglasses on sitting by the door. She had seen him there when she came in, but now realized he remained drinking one beer after another. Is he Texas-cool with those shades, she wondered? Certainly doesn't look Texas-friendly. Maybe he's blind and away from foot traffic to the bar and from the dancers-to-be.

Distracted by the old man, she was unaware that the band was starting to set up. Not much time needed for that with three players, she thought, and wondered without reflection if anyone in the bar noticed that she was alone. No one stared. No one gave her any sideways looks. No one cared.

The music ended with the smoke inside thick as cotton when Annie walked out to her car to drive to the other side of town to her room at the motel. For some reason, the two chain motels were at the *other* edge of town, two miles closer to the big city that was still 80 miles away.

Breath held, Annie got the Scout started without a shudder and drove the short distance to the motel. In the morning she would go see the lawyer who originally contacted her about this little bit of land and broken-down real estate that she'd inherited from a distant relation whom she thought dead for decades.

Uncle Ollie, as the kids always called him, was a dodgy character. Often drunk though never disorderly, he would still end up spending a night in the drunk tank after being brought to the jail by his own nephew, her father, the sheriff. One day, Ollie disappeared from town, and everyone, including her dad, thought he'd gotten himself in a stupor, fallen in the river, or been sucked under on a sandbar. The search her dad instigated produced no evidence, no body. A couple of months after his disappearance, they held a memorial service for him, and her dad placed a marker near his own mother's grave. Ollie's parents, long dead, were buried in a neighboring state.

In the decades that followed, Annie lost both her parents and most of her dad's people, as far as she knew. Then one day a letter arrived from a lawyer in a Texas town she'd never heard of with the revelation of her being Ollie's beneficiary. Although most men of Ollie's generation would have been predisposed to pass any fortune, large or small, to another male relative, Annie wasn't really surprised that she was his choice rather than her dad or her older brother. After all, it was always Annie, sociable and loquacious, who would take care of Ollie whenever her dad released him from a stint in the jail.

When Ollie was released after breakfast—he loved her mom's cooking—her dad would take him into his office and try to talk some sense into him, as her dad always insisted. Annie never failed to listen in from behind the door that separated her dad's office and the dispatchers from the family's quarters. When her father stopped talking, Annie would walk right into the office, take Ollie's hand, and lead him into the kitchen for another cup of coffee and one of her mom's famous cinnamon rolls. They'd sit there at the kitchen table, with her mother bustling around already working on the preparations for the prisoners' lunches. Annie would ask Ollie question after question, Ollie answering as best he could between bites of roll and sips of coffee. When a frown creased his forehead, Annie knew that it was time to get him two aspirin and say goodbye. Her father was always convinced that her time with Ollie did him more good than anything else.

I guess I benefitted more than Ollie in the long run, she concluded. Well, I'll sort out more of this mystery, perhaps, when I meet with the lawyer in the morning. Time for some sleep.

Next morning after she showered and dressed, she headed for the waffle-making table. Could waffles ever be truly bad, especially as the alternative to slimy boiled eggs and unidentifiable cereals in plastic containers? A waffle would also stick with her until after her 9AM meeting with the lawyer. Soon, she was driving down the winding street off the highway and into the town square. Lawyer Central, as she already called it.

"Ms. Thornton, Jim Hickok, no relation to Wild Bill," he smarmed. Oh, don't be a stereotype, please, Annie groaned inside and smiled outside.

"Thank you for seeing me this morning, Mr. Hickok."

"Jim, please." Less smarmy.

"What do we need to do?"

Thirty minutes later, the necessary papers were signed. The lawyer had also informed Annie that there was no bank account, but, of course, she could sell the land, if she wanted. He would be happy to help her find an agent, since she didn't know anyone in town. Annie smiled, nodded, and demurred. Then she walked out into the Texas summer sun.

"Already too late to avoid the heat." She didn't mean to say it aloud.

She drove back to Ollie's—now her—place. She put several fresh bottles of water on the counter in what passed for a kitchen and decided to look in that dilapidated shed that she'd seen yesterday. It sat slightly up the hill (she couldn't think of it as a mountain yet) from the old house. Wary of the ever-present spiders and snakes around the place, she proceeded very cautiously, pushing the rickety door wide enough to see in. Besides plenty of dust and cobwebs, only a few really old, worn-out tools leaned against the wall.

"I can't even imagine Ollie working on the land. Why did he disappear anyway? I know Dad felt he failed his family by 'losing Ollie.' I overheard him say that to mom more than once. And why did Ollie come here? And why not tell anyone? This is a long way from the town where Ollie lived most of his life, and Ollie never even owned a car." Her voice echoed in the hollow interior of the shed.

Annie exited the shed pulling the door toward her before walking back down the slight trail to the house. She stepped gingerly up the few steps and crossed the small porch into the house. The clutter inside included boxes filled helter skelter with papers, most of which had been shredded by mice. While she was in town, she had stopped at the convenience store and, besides the bottles of water, purchased some work gloves. Annie didn't plan to encounter any insect, rodent or other debris with her bare hands today as she sifted through the clutter.

Annie decided to work through the three rooms, one at a time. In the first room, she pulled one box toward her nearly knocking a framed photograph off the wall. It was hanging haphazardly but with the glass still intact over the photo.

"I have this same picture." She frowned and studied it carefully. "Yep, the same exact one, my dad and his deputies in the parking lot between the jailhouse and the courthouse. I didn't know Ollie had one, too."

She took her shirt tail and rubbed off the glass and the cardboard back. As she did, she noticed that on the back of the cheap frame, only one little metal wedge remained to hold the cardboard and photo in place. She turned the wedge slightly, freeing the cardboard on the back. Maybe I can get a better frame for this, she thought, as she took the cardboard away from the photograph. Then, Annie noticed writing on the back of the photograph.

She carefully removed the picture from the frame and carried it to make use of the light coming through the window. The writing on the back wasn't pretty or grammatically sound, but it was certainly more than a descriptive notation:

Samuel

I ben long gon when ya fine this picher I guess sorry I took it from yer office not tellin' nobody I ment to go and send it back onc't I settled but I'se two scared ben 30 year now mebbe I jest hold on to it a bit longer Annies gonna get my land and hous and belongins' when I'm gon so's ya no I got that little plaster pairs cat she gived me she sure could ask them questions jest like ya done as a boy she'll be a detectuv two sumday I sure do miss our mornin' visits sorry for the trubl

   Ollie

So that's how he got this picture, she thought. Dad never said a word about it being missing. I would have noticed, so Dad must have replaced it fairly quickly. That must have been at the same time Ollie disappeared. I guess Dad didn't think there was any connection. Why would Ollie want this photo? He loved Dad and spent plenty of time in the jail, but he never stole anything before. Not from us. What was Ollie scared of?

Her years as a researcher kicked in, and Annie pulled out her phone to take some pictures of the back of the photo and make some notes. Budget cutbacks throughout the university research unit where she worked had resulted in Annie's being let go from her position there shortly before she got word of the inheritance. The university administration had called it "hard decisions" in a budget crisis. But, she was glad to be out of that place that didn't value the difficult and necessary work she did. She feared at the time that her savings wouldn't last more than a year.

Too bad Ollie didn't leave me any money, she thought and immediately felt guilty. My god, girl, he gave you his land! What had the lawyer said, 10-12 acres? Maybe I should go through the stuff in the house—probably end up tossing most of it—then I can find a real estate agent to get the property on the market.

Yet even in her head, that sounded shitty. Ollie wanted her to have this place. He was so scared of something or someone that he disappeared without a word from the only family he had. Or was the disappearance of the photo a message? She looked down again at the writing on the back of the photograph and then at the photo.

But, what message, besides, 'sorry', she wondered? Thirty years and still scared. Of what? Could Ollie's junked-up house reveal something? Was there any point in sifting through all this debris?

A rustle in the corner of the room brought her out of her reverie. A mouse scurried along the baseboard for a few feet, taking shelter behind the broken down stove. She walked over to the stove and shouted, "Okay, mice, snakes, spiders, time to start moving out."

Four hours later, the sweat pouring into her eyes sent her out the door and back to town. The Purple Onion, the small cafe in town that closed at 3 o'clock, would be open for another 30 minutes, time enough to order take-out.

While she was driving into town, she realized that whatever she decided about the property was going to take longer than she originally intended. She thought of her former colleague and still best friend, Tessa, also out of work in the so-called budget crisis.

I'll call Tessa and beg her to come help me sort this out. It'll go a lot faster with two of us, she rationalized.

Tessa arrived that evening armed with dust masks, gloves, and two pair of short sleeved- coveralls, plus various cleaning supplies and a wet vac. Tessa always knew what was needed to get a job done, whether the job was repairing a 400-year old palimpsest or clearing out an old man's junked-up house.

Over beers and fajitas at The Edge of Town that night, Annie told Tessa all she knew about Ollie and his disappearance years before. It was a long story but still too short on details.

At the house the next morning, she showed Tessa the photograph and Ollie's sad note.

"What do you think it means, Annie?"

"I think he took the photo for a keepsake and was afraid to mail it back in case my dad told someone where Ollie was. And that someone told the wrong person."

"But, who could that 'wrong person' be? Any ideas at all?"

"Not really. Ollie was a benign old drunk who wouldn't hurt a fly. But, he did like to talk, or, when I was around, listen. Do you think he heard or saw something dodgy?"

"Sounds possible. Did he ever tell wild stories to you in your little talks?

"Well, he hardly got a word in. But, no, I don't remember anything strange. He did hang out at the pool hall. At least I remember my dad telling him that he shouldn't spend so much time there. Hard to imagine that now wholly gentrified strip with such a common thing as an old-fashioned pool hall. As a kid, I remember being shocked that my older brother went there when he was about sixteen. I didn't know any girls who went, except the, as my brother and his friends called them then, 'party girls'. What was that, a hundred years ago?"

Tessa laughed. "Such a place might be just the spot for seeing or overhearing something that would scare a drunk, old man, don't you think?"

"Possibly. Maybe we should work a couple of days on this place, see if anything else turns up that would give us a clue as to what happened. Then, go back to the city and dig through the county and city archives. Budget cuts have shortened their hours, but jobless, we can go during the few hours they're open, yes?"

"I haven't any bites from my job apps, so why not?"

The two set to work then, slowly sorting and tossing as they moved around the first room of the house exchanging a groan from time to time when a mouse ran into or out of a box.

Late summer light fading, Annie called to Tessa, "Hey, I found that plaster of Paris cat that I made when I was — what, eight? — and gave to Ollie."

"He mentioned it in that note on the back of the picture, didn't he?"

Tessa wiped sweat from her face as she spoke.

"Yes. I can't believe he kept it all these years. It looks pretty fragile now, but I am touched." Annie turned the little childish art piece in her hand and then looked at her friend. "Why don't we stop for the day and go back to the motel to clean up? Then we can find food and drink."

"Let me finish this box and then I'll be ready," Tessa shouted. "Wait, wait—I found something. Or nothing. Come see this!"

Annie almost tripped over a box she'd just emptied as she lurched across the floor to where Tessa stood, holding a key.

"Look."

"What kind of key is it?" Annie squinted in the half light of the room.

"I can tell you what kind it's not. Not skeleton, not padlock, not file key. Safety deposit box?"

"Maybe. Let me see. Yes, maybe, safety deposit box. But, shouldn't the lawyer have this in his possession?"

"Not if Ollie didn't give it to him." Tessa brought the key closer to her. "You never told me how he died."

"Because the lawyer never told me. He just said that his law firm drew up a will for Ollie, shortly before his death, bequeathing me all his property. But no one told me how he died, and, strangely, I never asked. I guess I assumed age and alcohol. Now I feel terrible about not asking. But, at the time, I really wasn't thinking about his death, only his life and disappearance. The lawyer creeped me out, too, so I wanted to come back out here, get things cleared up, and try to decide what I would do about it all."

"I suppose we'll have to wait until morning to reach anyone."

"It's too late for 9-to-3-ers, like the lawyer and the bank." Annie slipped the key into her coveralls.

They talked about the possibilities as they drove back to the motel to shower and change. No revelation seemed imminent from the tiny key. Annie put it into a pocket in her purse as they headed out the door to

The Edge of Town.

As their eyes adjusted to the interior of the ramshackle bar and grill, Annie saw the old—blind?— man, once again ensconced by the door. The only person he ever talked to, as far as Annie could tell, was the waitress. When Annie and Tessa sat down with their beer, Annie motioned to Tessa to lean over toward her.

"See that old guy with the sunglasses? He was here the other night when I first came in and stayed for the band. Remember, we saw him last night, too, when I mentioned seeing him before."

"Yes, so?"

"So, he was in that exact spot when I arrived and when I left after the band quit that first night and last night. Talking to no one but the waitress and keeping those sunglasses on in spite of being indoors, at night. I suppose he's some old eccentric or drunk, like Ollie."

"Is it possible that he knew Ollie?"

"I wonder? Ollie probably kept to himself, but, if he did go anywhere, this would be just his kind of place." Annie was thinking seriously about going over to the old man's table when he stood up and walked out the door. She knew better than to chase the old guy out into that dark, graveled lot. It was Texas. Everybody had a gun.

The next morning they delayed going out to the house early and instead went to the lawyer's office as soon as it opened.

"Is Mr. Hickok in?" Annie asked as she and Tessa walked toward the secretary's desk.

"Just in. Let me buzz him."

In a couple of minutes they were sitting in front of the lawyer's desk, and Annie produced the key. "Do you know if Ollie kept a safety deposit box?"

The lawyer eyed the key with clear skepticism and shook his head. "I wouldn't imagine so. I have to say, honestly, I'm surprised he made a will. He didn't strike me as someone, well, he didn't look—"

Annie interrupted his stutter, "—like someone who could pay a lawyer for anything?"

"Well, yes. But, he paid the bill promptly after we drew up the will, and that was it until a few weeks later when a woman, wanting to pick pecans on his property, saw his body through a window. The ambulance brought him to the morgue, and the sheriff contacted me since the county clerk had the deed to his place on file."

"I can't believe I didn't ask the first day I met with you but what was the cause of death? And where is he, um, his body?"

"Before we found you, we followed his instructions and had him cremated, his ashes spread over his property. Didn't I tell you that?"

"No. But I didn't ask. I guess because we "buried" Ollie long ago when he disappeared from our lives. Cause of death?"

"Let me see if I can find that in my notes in his file. Here it is. Congestive heart failure. Not uncommon in the old and infirm."

"Of course. Well, thank you for your time."

"Just let me know when you want that real estate agent's number."

Annie and Tessa walked out of his office in silence, but the minute they were in the car, Tessa turned to Annie with a frown, "So why's he pushing you to sell?"

"Is he? Well, he probably gets some referral fee or percentage from the real estate agency belonging to his brother or sister or some other relative. Let's go to the bank and see if Ollie has a box."

At the teller's window, Annie produced the key and asked if that key would be likely to open one of their safety deposit boxes.

"It's rather old and a bit rusty, but it might be one of ours. Is it yours?" asked the teller brightly.

"Yes. I inherited my…uncle's place recently and found this in the house. You can contact Mr. Hickok if you need to confirm my ownership of all the property." Annie was using her best professional voice with the teller.

"No, ma'am. I don't think that will be necessary. What's the name?"

"Ollie Griffith."

The teller turned to her computer and started hitting buttons. "Why, yes. Mr. Griffith has a box with us though he never opened an account here." Annie frowned slightly as the teller gave her a card and directed her to the other side of the lobby to an older woman sitting at a desk.

This woman *did* want to call Mr. Hickok's office so it was another fifteen minutes before Annie and Tessa were shown through the gated entrance to the room where the boxes were kept.

"I guess I'm not surprised that Ollie didn't keep any money in the bank since he was 'hiding out.' But, I am surprised no one accompanied us in here with a second key. Small towns, eh? The box number is A307." Annie was talking to her friend as her eyes scanned the numbers on the boxes.

"It's here, Annie." Tessa's voice hit a high note and then lowered on her friend's name. "Sorry, this is a little bit exciting. Makes me feel like we are in the archives again about to find the missing piece to one of our manuscript puzzles."

Annie put the key in the lock. "Here goes."

The key hesitated as Annie started to turn it but gave way and the lock clicked open. Annie pulled the box out and turned to the table in the center of the small room. "I feel nervous about this. Will there be something in this box that will tell us why Ollie ran away?" Annie held her breath as she opened the lid.

There were no papers, no money, only a single dusty cassette tape with Annie's name written on it in Ollie's scrawling, hesitant hand.

"Well, this is weird. I haven't seen a tape player at Ollie's yet. But my old Scout has one." Annie grabbed the singular contents of the box, replaced the box in the wall, and locked it.

The two walked swiftly out the gate barely acknowledging the "Thank y'all" from the woman at the desk.

Once in the Scout, Annie started it up and nervously fingered the cassette. "Now that we've rushed out here, I'm afraid to hear what's on this tape."

Speaking her fear out loud seemed to calm her as she slid the tape in the Scout's deck and hit "play." The tape started to turn with that well-remembered electronic sizzle before Ollie's voice came on:

"Annie. If y'all are hearin' this then I's dead. That's okay. Don't worry. Old and ready only regrettin' I didn't see y'all before I went. Sorry I didn't come home again. But, mebbe this here message will help y'all understand. The night fore I left home I's in the pool hall havin' a beer with my buddies. I felt the need to [pause] relieve myself and went on back. I's in the stall when the door op'nd up. I heard two men talkin' bout some other guy gettin' what he deserv'd. I stayed real quiet cuz they sounded mean. Well, one guy was sayin' that no one would ever know what happen'd cuz no body was gonna be found. Then the door creaked again and the two men shut up. A man come in whistlin' and kept on while he, well, you know. The other two musta walked out the door then as I heard nothing but that whistlin'. Then that was gone too. I shulda told your daddy that night. I did go to see him right after. But he weren't there. The night man let me set in your daddy's office to wait. I got so scared the longer I set there. Anyways, I took off without talkin' to your daddy. I run to my room and took the cash money my mama had left me and a bag a clothes and grabbed the first bus outta town. That bus stopped in this here little town and I never left again. I thought it better if no one knew what happen'd to me. That'd keep y'all safe. I bought the land with mama's cash and kept myself to myself mosta time. I am sorry about takin' your daddy's picher, but when I was waitin' in his office, I seen it there next to me on the wall, and, well, I just couldn't leave without...without some membrance of him. I took that little plaster pairs cat you made so I could member you, too. Sorry again. Member me with love, like I done you.

Annie wiped tears from her eyes before reaching over to turn off the player. Tessa stared at the glove compartment knob, unwilling to comment.

"That answers so many questions swirling in my head for the last, well, most of my life actually." Annie took a deep breath and turned to her friend.

"Poor old guy," Tessa felt for Ollie and her friend.

"To be afraid for all those years. So afraid that you never tell anyone. Recording this must have scared him all over again. I wonder when he did record this and how?" Annie puzzled.

"I wonder why he hesitated so long as he was talking about that picture he took? The one you said you found, right?"

"Yes. I wonder. Let's go back to the house and read his note again on the back of the picture." Looking in her side mirror, Annie slowly pulled away from the curb as she spoke.

When they got back to Ollie's place, they took the tape inside and went straight to the picture which now lay on the rippled linoleum that covered the kitchen counter. Annie picked it up and turned it over. They moved to a window to see Ollie's scrawling hand on the back.

Annie wrinkled her forehead and squinted at the lines. "He says that 30 years had gone by since he left and though he had already determined to leave me his property, he wrote this to my dad about sending the picture back. Out of guilt for taking it or some other reason?"

"And what's it have to do with his still being scared, as he says here?"

Tessa's question anticipated Annie's thoughts, and she looked at her friend. "Tessa, you're right, somehow this picture isn't just a remembrance but connected to what he overheard. The voices he heard. Did he know one of them or maybe both?"

Annie turned the photograph over and looked at the serious faces of her father and his deputies. "Is that a circle penciled in around this man's head?"

"It's ragged, but certainly a deliberate mark." Tessa lowered her head and tilted the picture more toward the window.

"I knew all dad's deputies. I used to play with that guy's little girl, Barbara; they lived just a few blocks away. What was their last name? Damn. Too many years have gone by."

"Keep thinking, Annie. Let's take it outside in full sunlight."

Annie held tightly to the photograph as they made their way out the front door and onto the rickety porch. She didn't think about snakes or anything but that photograph as she and Tessa stepped down to the weedy yard.

"Annie, look. This guy's head is circled, too."

"Wright."

"Right, about?"

"No, W-R-I-G-H-T. That was this deputy's last name." Annie pointed at the first circled head. "Looking at their pictures I can remember all their names now. This other man's name was…May. Jeff May. But, why draw a circle around these two? I wish Ollie had said more in his note on the back of Dad's photograph."

"Well, those deliberate circles meant something to him. Was he particular friends with these deputies?"

"No. They all knew Ollie, of course, but he just slept it off, talked with dad, and then I'd bring him into our kitchen. I don't remember him exchanging more words than necessary with any of the deputies."

"Let's set this aside and get through the rest of those boxes. Maybe we'll find something else. Another clue."

Annie smiled slightly at her friend as they went back inside.

They knew they were risking their health by going back to The Edge of Town for another fried dinner. By the time they cleaned up in their hotel room in the early evening, they didn't have the energy to drive the 30 miles to the nearest town with more restaurant choices. So back they went for more fried food and beers.

They ordered at the bar and settled into a table just as Texas Jambalaya started their first set. At the same moment, the old man in the sunglasses walked through the door and took his usual seat.

"Well, he likes the food and beer as well." Annie gestured more with her eyes than her head, and Tessa followed her gaze.

"I'm going to talk to him. Ask him if he knew your uncle. After we eat, of course."

"No. I should do that, but I don't know why I imagine he knew Ollie. And even if he did why he would know more than the lawyer or the bank."

They ate mostly in silence after their food came, watching a few people wander in for beer or a meal. But the music had ended and the bar had emptied out before Annie got up and walked toward the man by the door. Tessa didn't say anything to her friend but kept her eyes glued to Annie's back.

"Hi, there." Annie smiled and wondered if he could see or not.

"Mhmm."

"I, I'm Ollie Griffith's…niece…he died recently and I've come to clear out his place. I was wondering if you knew my Uncle Ollie?" She realized she should have said 'and pay my respects to his memory'.

"Mhmm."

"Oh, that's great. I mean it's nice to meet someone who knew my uncle. I hadn't seen him in a very long time. Did you know him well."

"Mhmm."

This was going to be tougher than Annie imagined. "So, did he come in here often?"

"Mhmm." Still the granite face, unseeing or not behind those glasses.

"Did he ever mention me, Annie? Oh, sorry, my name is Annie Thornton. And you are—"

"Stone."

Annie wasn't sure whether that was his last name or a description of his implacable nature. "Mr. Stone. Happy to meet you. How long were you...friends with Uncle Ollie?"

For the first time, the man shifted in his seat and turned slightly toward Annie. Did he see her? Was he going to get up and walk away? Annie's anxiety ratcheted up a notch, and her body stiffened, waiting for him to speak or move away.

He spoke. "I met Ollie when he first arrived. We was bar buddies. I never come to his place and he never come to mine. He come in here just fore he died and give me a letter for a little girl named Annie. I s'pose that's you, though you don't seem to be no little girl."

"No. I mean, I was when he last saw me. A letter?" Annie tried to keep her voice calm and steady.

"Here 'tis." The old man's arm moved slowly as his hand reached up and inside his shirt pocket. He held out a rumpled envelope.

"Thanks. Thank you, Mr. Stone. I'm grateful. But how did you know I'd come in to The Edge of Town?"

"Ya's Ollie's niece, ain't ya?" As he spoke the old man stood up and walked out the door.

Annie didn't move for a few minutes. She just stared through the cockeyed screen door into the darkness at the receding figure of the old man.

Because Ollie left that brief note on the back of the photograph, Annie could be sure that her name scrawled across the envelope was in Ollie's own hand. Pen marks with the same ink slashed through a printed return address. Annie recognized it as one of the envelopes in her dad's desk drawer when he was sheriff. The envelope was sealed, and by the look of it, had been for some time. She finally turned, letter in hand, and went back to the table where Tessa sat, literally on the edge of her seat.

"He was Ollie's friend, or drinking buddy, and he gave me this." Annie held the envelope up close to her chest and then put it in her bag.

Tessa nodded and stood up without a word. The two moved rather quickly out the old screen door, winding their way through the haphazardly parked cars until they reached Annie's Scout.

As soon as they were inside, doors closed, Tessa spoke. "Are you going to read it here now or when we get to the motel?"

"The light's too poor here. Would you mind if we did this at Ollie's house? I know it's creepy at night, but the electricity is on now, and I want to have this letter, the photograph, and the tape all together when I read it. Is that okay?" Annie peered at her friend through the scanty illumination of one, jury-rigged light attached to a pecan tree at the edge of the gravel lot.

"Yes, good idea."

They drove mostly in silence to Ollie's property, pulling in at the back of the house. Both women hopping out of the vehicle and making their way gingerly through the still too-tall grass in the pitch blackness surrounding the old house. Up on the porch, Annie removed the concrete block from the screen door, hoping no scorpions or snakes waited to strike within the recesses of the block. She switched on the single bulb in the kitchen area and then walked quickly into the other half of the open space to switch on the lamp sitting atop a small wooden table. A rather large chair covered with cracked faux-leather upholstery was positioned nearby. These two pieces and an old formica table with two chairs in the kitchen was all the furniture in the house. Annie brought one of the kitchen chairs over next to the faux-leather one nearer the lamp so they could both sit while she read the letter. Then Annie pulled the photograph from the drawer in the small table, the tape lying in her satchel on the floor.

When Annie and Tessa sat down, Annie immediately held the letter out to her friend. "I suddenly feel my nerves jangling. Would you open this and read it…out loud?"

Tessa took the envelope, turned it over in her hand, and then pulled a pocket knife from the bag at her feet. "It feels wrong just to tear it open."

Slitting the edge of the envelope with her knife, as carefully and reverently as she would the undivided pages of an early book, Tessa pulled the letter from inside and opened it. Her voice faltered so she cleared her throat and began to read:

little annie i shur am sorry not ta see ya again before i die but hope yer alone when ya read this

Tessa stopped reading and looked up at her friend. Annie's eyes blinking at her to go on:

if ya founded the picher i took from yer daddy's office that night and listened to m'tape then ya might be thinkin aready what im gonna tell ya — that night when i was in the toilet at the poolhall i knew them two voices and that's what feared me the most— they was too yer daddies deputees jeff may and ben rite tawkin as if they done killd somebudy —i drew a ring round the heads of them too in the picher— if they still round when ya get this ya tell ya daddy he knows what ta do
luv Ollie

Tessa stared at her friend waiting for Annie to speak first.

"Both of those deputies were shot and killed as they allegedly attempted to arrest members of a gambling ring. I remember my parents talking about it when Dad came home in the wee hours after it happened. I was maybe ten years old and woke up when I heard my dad's strained voice on the landing. I crept to the door of my room and listened. He said that both deputies were killed as they went into some warehouse or old barn to check out reports they'd heard about illegal gambling there. Dad said that everyone inside was dead when he and two of his other deputies arrived on the scene. The two Ollie mentioned and several of the 'gang', for lack of a better word. My folks went into their bedroom after that, and I didn't want to get caught sneaking around near their door. The two deputies' funerals were well-attended, and these two honored like fallen heroes. Oh, my god, that was only about two weeks after Ollie disappeared." Annie sat back in the chair feeling drained.

"Oh, Annie, Uncle Ollie could have come home then." Tessa's words echoed her own thoughts and sparked another memory.

"I caught my dad in his office one day staring out of his windows toward the courthouse. Maybe two or three days after the killings. I thought he was sad because of the death of those deputies, but when he turned toward me, I realized he was frowning. I'd call it a brown study now, but then I only saw worry and anger. I immediately felt a child's guilt even though I was sure I didn't do anything that day to make him unhappy. So, I went ahead and asked him what was wrong. Of course, he brushed it off—'Nothing, now go play.' I made a plan then, that whenever I knew he was in his office, I would suddenly need the bathroom which had two doors, one into the kitchen and one into Dad's office. A couple of days later, I heard him going into his office to pick up the phone. I ran to the bathroom and overheard him saying to someone on the other end that the crime scene didn't feel right to him.

Dad must have gone out there on his own that afternoon or with his attorney friend, Les Woodbridge. Les and Dad were good friends, and Les was not directly involved with Dad's department. Another few days went by before I saw Dad standing with Les on the front porch of the family quarters of the jailhouse. I cracked the window closest to the porch and squatted down beneath the sill."

"What did you hear then?"

"Les was saying it was no good at this point bringing up Dad's suspicions especially without rock solid evidence. Any scandal would reflect badly on Dad and his management of the department, never mind that the two deputies were crooked and probably involved with the gang."

"Holy, shit, Annie. Did you ever ask your dad about that, I mean, years later even?"

"No. Of course, none of us at the time connected that incident with Ollie's disappearance. I was just a kid, and kids tend to get caught up in their own concerns. And, neither Dad nor Mom ever referred to the killings again, not when I was near enough to hear anyway. Naturally, we made trips to the cemetery to visit family graves. Ollie's marker was next to my dad's mother and her other kin. We mourned and went on with our lives. But, no one ever voiced the possibility of any connection between Ollie's sudden disappearance and the deaths of May and Wright." Annie picked her satchel up off the floor. "Let's go back to the motel. I am suddenly really, really tired."

By morning, Annie knew what she must do with the letter, the tape, and the photograph with Ollie's note on the back. After breakfast in town, she explained her plan to Tessa as they walked over to the bank.

The woman who called the attorney to check up on Annie the first time remembered her, letting her go into the safety deposit box room with no more than a reminder to fill out a card for change of ownership. In the room alone this time, Annie went straight to Ollie's box and carried it to the table. She opened the lid and gently laid the three items into the box. Her hand lingered on the top of the lid as she closed it. No longer a safety deposit box, but a coffin, where Annie could lay Ollie and his fear to rest.

Shooting Pigs in Texas

For the first time in her life, Susanna Oswalda Schneider would have her own place. Not one she rented or part of a house that belonged to her mother or her grandmother, but a whole house with land and trees, and who knows what else, in a place she'd only heard stories about. On the Paluxy River in Texas.

She clearly remembered the stories about her grandmother, Alice, who had left her alcoholic husband, Oswald Martin, in Kansas and taken their six children south to Texas. Alice Martin's aunt on her mother's side had gruffly agreed to take them all in if Alice had the nerve to leave her husband. She did. The seven of them left for Texas within a week after her aunt's letter arrived.

Life was not easy for Alice, caring for six children and helping her aunt with her goats and the large garden. They milked the goats, made cheese and soap, and out of what seemed to Alice an endless garden, they canned and stored and traded with their neighbors. Although she worked incredibly hard, Alice felt the freedom from her drunk and abusive spouse, from worrying over what he might do to her children as they grew up and defied him. But, 'One did not divorce one's husband in those days', Susanna Oswalda recalled her mother telling her when relating stories of her own mother. And the reward came when Alice heard that her husband finally succumbed to years of drinking and fighting his way through life.

Without hesitation, Alice took her children back to Kansas to the house and farm she once occupied with Oswald Martin and that she now could claim as her own. Her oldest, Sarah Jane, old enough by then and having her own mind, stayed with her great aunt in Texas and continued milking the goats, making the cheese and soap, canning the garden veggies, and trading with the neighbors for other essentials.

That impressed Alice, though it didn't make her happy. She missed her stubborn, independent-minded daughter very much. Later, when Sarah Jane's first child was born in Texas, Alice Martin insisted that her daughter name the little baby girl, Susanna, after Alice's aunt, the woman who had taken Alice and her children in all those years ago. Sarah Jane complied, but, with her own brand of stubbornness, Sarah Jane also perversely gave her child a middle name sure to make Sarah Jane's mother mad. Oswalda. The diminutive of her father's name. A name Alice Martin never allowed to be mentioned in her hearing.

But that wasn't the end of the name game for poor little Susanna Oswalda Schneider. One of her grandmother's siblings, who knew plenty about Susanna Oswalda's grandfather, Oswald Martin, started calling that little baby girl "Ozzie."

At two, little Susanna "Ozzie" Schneider was already a fighter, though only drunk on her own independent nature. The name stuck nonetheless. After Sarah Jane's husband died when a tractor he was working on collapsed on top of him, she finally heeded her mother Alice's call to return to Kansas with Susanna Oswalda and her baby brother in tow. By that time, Susanna was as stubborn as her mother and grandmother. She even called herself "Ozzie" though only out of her grandmother's earshot. When Ozzie started school, the kids quickly discovered that, besides her oddly boyish middle name, her initials provided them another hysterically funny bit of fodder for their own jokes— S.O.S. Not unlike her grandfather, Susanna Oswalda "Ozzie" Schneider might have to be fighting her way through life.

On this, her second day on the Paluxy River in Texas, a fully adult "Ozzie" Schneider stood outside the old shotgun house. Once her grandmother's refuge, it now belonged to Ozzie herself. Great aunt Susanna had taken in Ozzie's grandmother and her children and then bequeathed the place to the child that stayed when Alice went back to Kansas, the eldest, Sarah Jane, Ozzie's mother. Sarah Jane hadn't needed or wanted to live in Texas again but held onto the house and land, later settling it on her eldest child, Ozzie.

Maybe her mother thought of it as recompense for Ozzie's being called after her drunken grandfather. For whatever reason, Ozzie now had a place where she could call herself Susanna or Oswalda or Ozzie or S.O.S. or whatever the hell she wanted. As she stepped off the porch and walked along her own road in the dust and the Texas heat, she felt fully in control of her name and her life. But, by her obstinate nature and perverse nurture, she introduced herself to the postmistress in the little tiny drive-through town nearby as "Ozzie."

The chatty, informative post mistress had told Ozzie another story, a much sadder one even than Alice Martin's. The post mistress related the story of the last Indian in Texas, shot on the property Ozzie just inherited. This poor soul, the postmistress assured her, was buried in a small, cemetery across the highway from the end of Ozzie's long gravel road. Ozzie suspected it was just a good Texas story to get her curious enough to investigate and report back to the post mistress. But, here she was, striding down her long, dusty, gravel road toward the highway and that graveyard.

She reached the edge of the highway and peered carefully in both directions before crossing over. The hot sun beating down on the back of her neck the moment she emerged from the protective shade of the trees along her road. No trees survived between where the edge of her property met the highway and that cemetery nearly a quarter of a mile along the other side where another narrow gravel road ran east and west. The glare of the sun and the heat that now enveloped her were merciless.

Ozzie walked a short distance west down that second gravel road and then veered off to the south into the cemetery. No fence, no gate, no sign marked it, just odd rectangular gravestones sitting here and there over about a hundred square feet of ground. Road aster, which seemed to thrive in the harsh Texas sun, now enveloped the stones, most of which sat cockeyed rather than upright, the markings hard to decipher. One stone, lying flat against the ground and some distance away from the gathering of the other stones caught Ozzie's eye. She moved toward the area where this odd stone lay. Ozzie squatted down to attempt to read its markings. All she could make out was the inscription of a year that put it in the realm of possibility as the grave she wanted to find. She stayed bending down over the stone for a long time before she was satisfied that she actually could read the date, while her imagination created yet another story of a life that once was.

A mockingbird singing its repertoire of stolen song brought Ozzie upright. She thought for a moment that she was surrounded by a variety of birds before she remembered the Texas mockingbird. Ozzie stood over the grave in the neglected cemetery for another moment with sweat pouring into her eyes and sliding down under her breasts. Soon, she turned to hike back along the dusty path and across the highway to her own road. Ozzie's head still buzzing from the songs of the mockingbird and the heat, she suddenly remembered the pigs.

The family stories about her grandmother's, and even her mother's, years in Texas never failed to mention the pigs. Ozzie couldn't remember the pigs, since she was so young when they left, but the pigs fascinated her as did her grandmother's Texas life, a life that Ozzie used to think must have been hard and lonely. By the time she was in her 30s, Ozzie realized the difference between being alone and being lonely.

Ozzie more often than not chose being alone to being in a group. She was most content on her own. Consequently, when Ozzie set out to explore her newly acquired property early in the morning on her second day there, she thought only of the days she had spent imagining her grandmother's life in a place she now called her own. Ozzie found everything here utterly captivating.

The heat stroke that Ozzie felt certain was coming on as she walked back along the highway, subsided in the shade trees at the gate. Staying in the shade on her property, Ozzie found herself skirting the Paluxy River running nearby.

The high banks of the tree-lined Paluxy were strewn with stones washed up from the rare times rain drenched the hard Texas earth enough to flood the river. The river itself was just a relative trickle in late August, meandering slowly along the bottom of the V formed by the high banks.

The house, the fields, and the river made Ozzie aware of the freedom that her grandmother must have felt.

She crossed the river now and wandered through the fields that neighbors recently mowed and baled after Great-Aunt Susanna died. Ozzie was making a mental note to talk to the postmistress about hiring someone to mow and bale, when, suddenly, she found herself surrounded by the pigs. At first, she felt no impulse to panic. After all, her other grandfather back in Kansas used to keep pigs. Ozzie remembered only one bad run in with them.

One hot summer day, she and her brother crossed paths with a sow and her piglets. Both children were less than ten at the time and, though farm-tough, no match for that sow. On that hot day at their grandparents' farm, Ozzie's little brother assured her that their mother gave him permission for the two to go down through the pasture and take a dip in the horse trough by the windmill. They were barely wet when that sow and her piglets surrounded the trough to wallow in the cool mud along its edges.

Fortunately for Ozzie and her brother, the sow couldn't get in over the sides of the trough. That old sow wasn't about to let the human piglets get out though. All they could do was scream for their mama and hope she heard them. She did. And, rescued them. And, gave them a good licking for scaring her and upsetting the mother pig and her babies.

The creatures surrounding Ozzie at this moment, she realized, were ten times the size of that angry sow. Ozzie considered it prudent to slowly back away and ease herself toward the river. She had only taken a few steps, when a monstrous boar emerged from the herd and charged.

Ozzie was in the middle of the river, ankle deep in water and shaking, before her eyes focused enough to see that the boar had stopped at the edge of the steep embankment, looked suddenly indifferent, and headed back to his herd. She imagined that he raised his large snout and gave a snort when he turned as if to say, "and stay there"! She didn't wait to see if he changed his mind. Ozzie clambered quickly up the opposite bank, running her best time into the house.

When she regained the relative safety of her small house, Ozzie showered and changed. Recovered from the pigs and the heat, she resumed unpacking the boxes that covered most of the floors in the three rooms that were the house. In spite of, or maybe, perversely, because of, her encounter with the pigs, Ozzie's comfort level rose again as she began to unpack—clothes and bathroom items, kitchen things, and sheets. The blankets wouldn't be needed until probably mid to late October, or so she had been told by her local news source, the postmistress. It would take some adjustment to her body's more northern expectations, but she thought she'd manage just fine. She was looking forward to a sunny autumn and winter in her new place.

As she worked to unpack her boxes, the heat reasserted itself. One tiny AC unit in the bedroom wasn't going to cool this house, as small as it was. Ozzie's experience of briefer, but equally intense, summer heat in Kansas was sufficient to make her see the futility of that little window unit. It was pointless to turn it on until an hour before she went to bed. Ozzie, keen on making her small savings go a long way, was naturally frugal like her mother and grandmother. But, when she inherited this house, in a place mostly remembered fondly in her imagination, she didn't hesitate to quit her job and withdraw her savings, eager to experience life in earnest on the Paluxy River in Texas.

She dug around in one of her boxes until she found her old desktop fan. It didn't put out much air, but a little breeze was better than none. Once the fan was going, she continued pulling out this and that until she came to the boxed contents of her cedar chest.

The "hope chest," that her mother gave Ollie for her twelfth birthday. The conventional "I-hope-I-get-married" chest in those days. Over the next few years, it was filled by her mother with doilies and dishes and crocheted baby booties and tea towels and all the other items that a working-class bride should have as an offering, the remnant of a time when every female must come with a dowry or not come at all. Later, enlightened by real life, Ozzie filled the chest with birthday and Christmas cards, cards of friendship and love, mementoes of all sorts from friends and lovers worth remembering. The inevitable musings over every memory that each keepsake evoked consumed the rest of the daylight.

Even after the sun was long down, the heat remained. Sweat continued pouring into Ozzie's eyes as she worked. Near midnight, another mockingbird, whose natural rhythms were obviously askew, piped away in a tree right outside her bedroom window, suddenly dislodging her mental meanderings enough to remind Ozzie to turn on the little AC unit. An hour or so later, she decided to try to get some sleep. She really wanted to be up early enough to finish the last bit of unpacking before she headed back to the post office for a chat with that most illuminating postmistress. Ozzie had plans.

She intended to return this place to a goat-cheese-and-soap producing "ranch" with a healthy truck garden for trade. Ozzie had more than her tough great aunt's first name. Susanna Ozzie Schneider had the pugnacity of her granddaddy along with the stubborn streak of her mother and grandmother. And Ozzie was alcohol- and husband-free.

In her bed, Ozzie turned her body away from the window and buried one ear in her pillow. But, even with the AC unit running, she could still hear that lone mockingbird in the tree. As the bird gave a mournful trill, like a dove, Ozzie shut her eyes trying to concentrate on the low hum of the AC. She continued moving around in the bed, attempting to drive the bird song from her head. Then the sudden silence of the mockingbird brought her fully awake. That and the sound that took its place.

The pigs were right outside her house. Their grunting and shuffling disturbed Ozzie more than she might have imagined. Her mother never wanted to talk about the pigs. Her grandmother supplied just enough description of the beasts to fire Ozzie's active imagination. Grandma Alice always said that these pigs had no natural predators except humans, the cause of the wild herds in the first place.

After her grandmother's death, when Ozzie was in her early teens, she tried to get her mother to talk more about the pigs, but Sarah Jane still refused. After Ozzie inherited this place, she fired up her laptop to see if she could find more information about Texas. In the process, she discovered the history of Texas's feral pigs.

According to several sources, the Spanish brought the ancestors of these pigs to Mexico and then Mexican settlers traveled with their domesticated herds into Texas. Later, the Anglo settlers took full advantage of the food source provided by the herds of wild pigs evolving from the domestic ones left to roam before and after the Mexican settlers were displaced by the Anglos. But apparently, the wild pigs' reproduction outpaced that of their human predator. Now, the sound of the descendants of those first wild pigs stopped the mockingbird's song and disturbed the gentle hum of the air conditioner. The sounds the pigs made reminded her of Donald Sutherland's character in "The Invasion of the Body Snatchers," mouth open, screeching, invading. And, apparently, standing right outside Ozzie's window.

Grandma Alice once told Ozzie that Great-Aunt Susanna believed in two methods of dealing with these pigs. If one or two wandered across the river, she would shoot at them with an inadequate .22 rifle as she did any garden pest. Although the .22 shot only made these bruisers mad, the sound of the indirect fire was effective enough to run them off. When the whole herd came calling, Great-Aunt Susanna's other method was to hide everyone. She put her goats in the little barn and the dogs, kids, Alice and herself in the house barring the doors. She let the pigs have their way with her garden. It happened infrequently enough in those days. And her great aunt hated asking anyone else for help. Ozzie, on the other hand, wanted any help she could get where the pigs were concerned.

Lost in the sounds of the feral pigs, Ozzie nearly jumped out of the bed when her cat, Sadie, landed next to her head. Ozzie's startled movement scared the cat so that she leapt down off the bed almost without having touched it, verifying the term 'shotgun' for this long, narrow house. This bit of normal wildness, however, had the effect of disconnecting Ozzie from her musings and the pigs.

Ozzie awoke breathing hard, her head pounding, her skin covered with fine, small beads of sweat. She lay still until her breathing had slowed and become more regular. She reached out for Sadie, who always slept right next to her, but Sadie wasn't there. Ozzie sat up with no sense of the time and struggled a bit to locate her clock. 4AM. The rush of adrenaline from that slowly-evaporating dream and anxiety over the whereabouts of Sadie forced her completely out of bed. "Sadie, dammit." Ozzie nearly fell as she twisted herself away from the cat on the floor by the bed. After that, Ozzie padded barefoot into the kitchen to put the kettle on. She couldn't quite shake the remnants of dream and sleep that kept her head throbbing, lightly but persistently, until she finished her tea with an added spoonful of sugar to clear her head.

Although having been aroused earlier than she'd wanted, when the sun's rays slanted across her floor, Ozzie was busily sifting through her boxes. Sadie, hoping for a second breakfast, wound through her legs every time Ozzie carried a pile into the kitchen.

The dream that robbed Ozzie of sleep vaguely haunted her as she worked, but it was too unreal. Deftly dodging the cat, Ozzie started out the door with her arms full of deconstructed boxes when she heard the sounds of her dream.

Pigs were real.

Ozzie's body stiffened. She slammed the door and dropped the boxes on the floor. Then she walked quickly back to the bedroom. The modest cabinet in the corner held only one object so far, another keepsake. It was a small caliber rifle, painted canary yellow, the one thing she had of her grandfather's. Ozzie only wanted it because having it annoyed her grandmother. She hated guns and shooting since nearly killing a squirrel with her brother's .22 after he badgered her into going hunting with him one day. Ozzie wouldn't even kill spiders when they invaded her space. Instead, she would catch the trespassing spider under a glass, slip a thin piece of cardboard beneath spider and glass, and release the spider outside.

Now Ozzie stood inside her house facing the Paluxy. The sounds of the pigs emanated from some place between the river and her house. Slowly, she moved toward the window. Ozzie saw four or five pigs rooting around the ground in the space where she planned to renew the garden. One particularly large boar lifted its head toward the house as if he heard her moving there. She lifted the rifle to her shoulder and aimed at his head. She knew that boar and his porcine gaze.

She looked down the barrel. Right between his piggy eyes. "Who's the predator now?" she whispered as she held the rifle level and stared down the barrel at the boar.

Suddenly, a mockingbird flew across her sights, dislodging the murder in her. The barrel of the gun drooped as she lowered it and returned it to the closet.

Ozzie turned her attention back to settling into her house and making plans for her goats and her garden. Tomorrow she would visit the chatty postmistress again to ferret out the name of a local trapper. Wild boar was a delicacy at fine Texas restaurants everywhere.

Agneta Agonistes

F leischer Dairy, Lancaster, Kansas
    Saturday -December 31, 1955
    Temp. 33° at 7 P.M. Cistern empty.

Lucinda brought Gerry home at 8.45. ~~He didn't want to go to basketball game at 9.~~ *David & Edwards* ~~patrol & watch dancing parties~~ ^{supervised} *at Community Bldg. Gerry doesn't like the Sheriff idea for his Dad. Jennie made bread tonight. At 11P.M. Janice and Harland Mueller came out, had coffeebread, coffee & cocoa Sylvie at Collins* ^(until 2:30AM!!) *Collins's took Jana & Bob Hodgkiss to K.C. to take plane to Rose bowl game. To bed at 12.30. Read my novel. Nice day.*

Every morning, Agneta reread her diary entry from the night before. Pen still upraised, she was pondering her corrections to the last entry, wondering how much interpretation she should allow herself, when she realized her daughter would soon be interrupting her thoughts to bring her lunch. Her daughter, Jennie, ran a tight ship with three children and a husband running for Sheriff that year. But Agneta harbored a certain amount of resentment over the rigor of her days and nights, over her dependence on Jennie.

"Curse these useless limbs," Agneta spoke softly but aloud as she put down her pen, closed her diary, and cleared the space in front of her on the table. "I suppose she is doing her best to keep up with all the schedules and to make sure that I get what I need." Agneta sometimes thought her daughter Jennie more an Älva, dancing along the mist above the ground, for good or ill purposes; Agneta could not be certain.

As if on cue, Jennie came gliding into view with a bowl of hot oyster stew in hand, Agneta's favorite oyster crackers floating on top. "Coffee's coming right up, Mother," she said in that tired but efficient voice which particularly annoyed Agneta.

"Thank you, Jennie." Agneta wanted a glass of fresh milk, too, but dared not ask for something that Jennie hadn't anticipated.

Without admitting it even to herself, Agneta rather enjoyed watching the reaction when she even slightly disrupted her daughter's well-planned routines. Agneta was sure that she could see the sigh as it moved up from Jennie's diaphragm, swelling her chest and closing her eyes as it emerged in a gust from her lips.

Jennie needs to be more flexible or she'll burst, Agneta thought as she curled her aching, arthritic fingers tightly around the handle of her soup spoon.

Her fingers were bowed from the joint above the knuckle by the arthritis that had bent her whole body into a sitting position seventeen years ago. Pain was a constant in her life. Though the daily doses of aspirin helped, they didn't completely stifle it. Jennie had been blamed by her siblings for crippling their mother; Agneta had known they tormented Jennie but hadn't been able to stop them altogether. The boys locked Jennie in the milk cooler so often she became terrified of tight spaces. To this day, she couldn't even wear a blouse with a tight collar.

Jennie had been a hard delivery on that dark, cold February night.

Born at 2AM on John's birthday, she immediately became a daddy's girl. The doctor had taken his sweet time getting there even though her anxious husband had called him when it became clear that Agneta was in trouble. Jennie was the sixth child, and they hadn't expected any complications. But Agneta wasn't the young, athletic woman she had been when her first child had arrived sixteen years earlier.

A child had been born nearly every two years after three miscarriages in the first few years of their marriage, and only Agneta's stubborn resistance to her husband's physical demands had prevented more children in fewer years. Agneta's mother was with her for the first child and had insisted that Agneta let her do all the domestic chores, including tending to the new baby for the first weeks. But, with each child and the subsequent inactivity, Agneta retained more of the inevitable weight of pregnancy. Over those childbearing years, Agneta became heavier and more lethargic which made it easier for her to repel her husband's increasingly infrequent conjugal advances. After Jennie was born, Agneta intended to have no more children. *I was too old to have more babies,* she told herself again. *John couldn't have expected me to continue indulging his appetite with six mouths to feed.*

The memory of these quarrels made Agneta shudder. Yet she struggled, as usual, to dismiss thoughts of her late husband.

Fleisher Dairy, Lancaster, Kansas
  Sunday - January 1, 1956
  Temp. at noon 49° at 9P.M. 34. Real sharp wind all day.

Up at 8.45. New brown dress (Lu&Albert). David out until 4A.M. Edwards with HW patrol. I slept good all night. Listened to church service. Dan Page sang beautiful solo then preached the sermon. Extra good. David slept until others came from church. Boiled ham, potatoes, and cabbage, good New Year's Sunday supper.

Writing the new year's date usually gave Agneta hope for the year to come. But as she finished writing this January 1st entry, she didn't feel very hopeful. She would be 74 in February near the birthdays of her three daughters. How had that happened, she wondered? Did John's demands come at a certain time each year? All the girls born in February, all the boys in August. Agneta wrinkled her brow as she made the calculations. Counting back from Jennie's birthday, Valentine's Day, she knew meant conception had occurred in mid-May. For the boys, whose birthdays are a few days apart in August, early November.

What was I thinking, feeling, imagining? I can't remember. I understand the practicality of carrying in the winter, but who would deliberately plan to be in the last aching months of pregnancy in the heat of summer? Still, we had three boys and three girls in a perfect, boy-girl pattern. So strange now to have no memory of planning. Perhaps I relented in the first blooms of early summer and the first cold nights of winter. So long ago.

She had thought about John often during the year since his death. And she resented spending her time hashing over memories and motivations. But did she resent him or herself? With the first anniversary of his death fast approaching, she flipped backwards in her diary to confirm the date.

Yes, we lost him the 26th of this month, she remembered and then chastised herself. That's enough sentiment. Get on with your work.

The sunshine flooded the room where Agneta worked her crosswords, crocheted, read, wrote in her diaries, took her meals, and slept. Her room was the formal dining room of the old farmhouse. John had converted it into their bedroom when Agneta lost the use of her legs. Thanksgiving and Christmas dinners were still served on the walnut dining table in that room, but the rest of the time, it was filled with Agneta's crocheting paraphernalia, her books, her diary, and various papers.

After she was crippled by the arthritis, John had slept there with her and even taken his supper at the table with her. But he insisted on wheeling her into the kitchen for breakfast with the family each morning. In the last few years before he died, he could no longer sleep with her nor push her chair. Another bed had been fitted into the corner of the room next to hers, the living room. He had died on that bed, and she had known the minute he was gone.

Through the open passage from dining room to living room, she could hear her ailing husband moving restlessly in his bed that night. Jennie had insisted that her mother go to bed at the usual time. She, Jennie, would be there next to John through the night. Agneta came awake abruptly, feeling as if someone were standing over her but unable to see clearly in the half-light of that January morning. As she reached full consciousness, Agneta heard Jennie calling, "Daddy! Daddy!" Agneta closed her eyes and waited. But, of course, Jennie had not come to her mother then. Instead, she stumbled up the stairs to her sleeping husband.

Later, Agneta heard David coming down the stairs. He told her what she already knew that her husband of fifty years was gone. David assured her that John had died in Jennie's arms. Hoping that was a comforting fiction for Agneta. It was not.

Agneta hadn't cried until David left her to begin the arrangements, to telephone Agneta and John's other children. Alone, she wept quietly but without relief for a long time. She wanted to say something, anything, but, there was nothing to say. Not to David or Jennie or their children who were about to get up for school. Or, poor little Jessie, Agneta thought.

The youngest of David and Jennie's three children, Jessie idolized her grandfather who reciprocated fully. Jessie, so little, not yet four, would not willingly be separated from her grandfather every day. Until the last month when John took to his bed. Even then, Jessie would sit for hours every day talking to him and to her grandmother after Jennie wheeled Agneta into the living room next to John's bed. Agneta heard the thump above her the morning John died, which meant Jessie was on her way down to see her grandfather.

"Grampah!" Jessie called out. Agneta listened to the little feet bouncing down the stairs and caught her breath before she heard Jennie rushing out of the kitchen to intercept the child. Too late, Agneta thought.

Agneta remembered Jessie sitting that deathly morning, cross-legged and crying in the middle of the kitchen table, until her pajama top was soaked with tears.

Asking questions even as she cried. "Where is Grampah? Who took him? Why would God do that? I don't want him to read stories to children in heaven. I want him to read to me!"

Agneta knew that it had driven Jennie wild, caught up as she was in controlling her own grief. Jennie not only loved her children without reservation, but, even though she had idolized her father, once childishly believing him invulnerable to sickness and death, Jennie understood what he had meant to Jessie. So Jennie kept her own grief largely to those times when she could be alone or only with David.

The two older children, who did understand death, cried their tears and went on with the distractions of school and friends. Little Jessie was too young for both and found comfort only in two things—the stories her grandmother told her about her grandparents' courtship and marriage or their ancestors in Sweden, and her animals.

Jessie wandered the yard and garden area around the house with her dog, Britta, and the two cats, talking to them and to her horse, Blue, who was allowed to wander in the acre around the house. She also played with her only doll in the playhouse David had built when Jessie's older sister, Sylvie, was small. But she always preferred her critters to dolls.

As winter gave way to spring, the playhouse and the big tree whose branches hung over it became Jessie's refuge from the house where her grandfather had died. Her dog had a litter of ten puppies early that summer, and the lively puppies, with all her other animal best friends, helped Jessie get through the first summer without her grandfather. The first of the rest of her life, Agneta thought, hoping Jessie's life would be long and happy, her own mercifully short.

These melancholy thoughts held Agneta on and off throughout the interruptions of the day—meals, afternoon coffee with visitors, a card game, more visitors. The activities alleviated the memories that washed over Agneta but did not take those memories away. Agneta managed to divert herself from time to time by brooding over one trivial thing or another, like her daughter Dorothea's oldest girl's poor choice of boyfriends. But that wasn't, if Agneta were to be honest, terribly interesting.

Janice wanted to be married but was not yet out of high school. Agneta could imagine that once Janice graduated and went to college, her education would be sacrificed to the first decent boy who wanted to marry her. Janice was sweet and always kind to her grandmother. Agneta had never been sentimental about her own children but revealed some sentimentality toward her grandchildren. Agneta was willing to show her affection more readily with the latter. She didn't fool herself, as she believed other parents or grandparents did, into thinking her progeny were more than they were.

Unlike Janice, Agneta had never thought of marriage. Marriage had been the frightening specter hovering in the harsh outlines drawn from her own parents' troubled marriage, their arguments always audible through the thin walls of the house. Although she heard the other young girls sigh over one boy or another and in later years contemplate becoming a wife, Agneta had never sighed over a boy or considered becoming a wife herself. Until she met John.

Why does every meditation come back to John? Meeting John, marrying John, living with John, watching his muscular, erect frame slowly bend as my own body grew fat and immobile, she demanded. Trapped in this chair, in this body, in the past. I can almost hear my son's wife Miriam's Pollyanna voice, "Mother Fleischer, you have so much to be grateful for, look at this family. I was an orphan. I know suffering and lack of love. Until I met Joseph, I didn't know what real love was. Count yourself lucky, Mother."

Yes, I am lucky. Lucky to have had a man like John to love me, to stay with me, to put up with me, to take care of me all those years, to give me six living children who are good in their own ways. But not so lucky as to have escaped my mother's teachings, she realized.

Her mother had drummed it into her head from the time she was a young girl: "The physical act of marriage is degrading and disgusting. It is necessary only for bearing a child, Flicka. Only bad girls find pleasure in that filthy act," her mother lectured endlessly as Agneta matured. A lesson Agneta had taken to heart only too well. What she never admitted even to herself was the tension in her own parents' marriage caused by her father's heavy drinking. Or was his drinking a result, she often wondered?

Whenever Agneta's husband had wanted to make love to her after the first child had been conceived, she deflected his touch with a most effective weapon, her mother's little dictum: "It is only for making a child." She put him off as long as possible after each child was born even as her own body ached for him. She rejected her desires and his. Only the dreams of this last year, after his death, had given him back to her in ways she had never allowed herself or him when he lived. He often came into her dreams, and in those dreams, and only there, came the true expressions of what she felt for John. Her heavy face sagged visibly as she remembered the dream of the night before.

"Mother, what are you doing? You're going to spill your soup if you don't put that spoon down," her daughter's brisk, business-like voice broke through her reflections like a gunshot.

"I was trying to remember…what was the exact day your daddy died," Agneta said almost convincingly.

"It was the 26th, Mother." Jennie still worshipped her father and frowned at his wife's apparent lapse of memory, and, she was certain, real feeling.

Jennie and her mother, though sharing an overall practical nature, were very unlike in most other ways. Jennie was a passionate wife and mother, given to physical demonstrations with husband and children in spite of her practical penchant to keep everyone organized. The real reason for her mother's momentary lapse would never have occurred to Jennie or been believed, if it had. In Jennie's estimation, her mother had always spent too much time with her books and papers. Agneta was a reader and a thinker and took time out of every day to read and to write in her diaries, even before her disability as she efficiently performed the hard and thankless chores of a farmer's wife. Jennie had never witnessed any overt demonstrations of affection from her mother.

Jennie had not been fussed over with affection or attention. Even when she or one of her five siblings was ill, while caring for them most effectively, their mother never stroked their feverish brows or catered to their childish whims. No blatant demonstrations of affection for her children, her husband, or anyone else as far as Jennie knew. Jennie didn't think Agneta was emotionally empty or cold. After all, she had done all that was required to physically care for her family but would not even kiss the children goodnight after the nightly story Agneta insisted upon reading. Nor would she hug them spontaneously or respond to their own artless demonstrations of affection. Agneta gave her family her best and expected the same from them. She doted on no one.

Well, Jennie thought, Mom does let the children hug and kiss her as they wish and smiles at them as they do. That's more than she did for us, her own children. Mother has no problem telling her grandchildren that she's proud of even their smallest, childish achievements.

Jennie could recall only one puzzling moment in her own childhood when she came around the corner of the house near the garden. Her mother stood in the vegetable garden. Jennie could just see the side of her face. Agneta was smiling at the receding figure of her husband as he walked away from the garden toward the fields. Jennie only thought it odd that her mother stared so but, as a child, did not think much more about it.

She realized now that she never thought about her mother as an active person—standing in the garden, bending down over the hoe, pulling the weeds, tending the first shoots of the vegetables grown every year, cooking, canning. Jennie associated none of these with her mother. It was her older sister, Magdalene, who ran the household for as long as Jennie could remember.

Mother had been there, certainly, but always in the shadow of Magdalene's dictatorial and orderly running of them all, Jennie recalled. Maybe that's what struck me most that day in the garden, seeing Mother standing outside rather than sitting with her mending or shelling peas or some other sedentary chore. I've always thought of mother as a woman gradually bending under the weight of disease and age. Not working in the garden. Except that one time, so long ago.

When Jennie returned to live with her parents after David shipped out at the start of the Second World War, she allowed the years to be consumed raising her children and tending both of her parents in their physical decline. Her father suffered for years from a heart condition which he denied having. Her mother was confined to a wheelchair by the time Jennie graduated from high school. Now Agneta was just another of the children whom Jennie fed, bathed, took to the toilet, and put to bed.

Though Jennie was bright and capable, she was not a deep thinker. If she couldn't resolve an issue with a practical solution—baking a cake for a grieving friend, sewing a dress for her oldest daughter's next recital, putting iodine on yet another cut or scrape acquired by her two youngest—it wasn't worth thinking about. It was God's will or couldn't be helped or changed by anything *she* could do. She worried only over the solutions to practical problems not over abstractions with no resolution.

Maybe mother is getting senile, she thought. After all, she is an invalid and, if it weren't for David's willingness to lift her into the car and take her for a drive once in a while, Mother would never leave the house. Her mother's scrutinous gaze pierced her thoughts so Jennie pulled herself out of that dangerous abstract territory.

"Mother, do you need anything else? I'm getting ready to start my bread making."

"No, thank you. I'm fine." Agneta finished her soup and coffee and pushed the dishes as far as she could toward Jennie's already outstretched hands. Agneta also was ready to have her work space cleared for her latest project.

She loved crocheting because she was good at it, and it kept her bent hands moving. She was convinced that they ached less when she crocheted a few hours every day. After she finished the potholder she was working on, Agneta would read that new novel that Miriam brought the other day. But, she realized that Jennie's two oldest, Gerry and Sylvie, would be coming home from school soon and come running into her room with a "Hullo, Grammah," a quick kiss on the cheek, and a recital about their school day. The baby, Jessie, popped in throughout the day for a story or a family history lesson or sometimes just to sit with Agneta and draw a picture. The rest of the time Jessie was running about outside in all types of weather with her dog and the old brood mare David had acquired to prevent the horse being destroyed when her foaling days had ended.

He was a soft touch for animals and children, and Agneta considered him a fine asset to the family. When David and Jennie had eloped without consulting Agneta and John, Agneta was sure John would never forgive David. In a very short time, John came round to appreciating David's good nature and his devotion as a husband and father.

What other man would have moved into his in-laws' home after his discharge without a ripple of complaint or ungraciousness? They clearly needed his and Jennie's help. After all, they had taken his wife and the first two children in when he was sent overseas in the last year of the war. He knew that, practical and efficient as she was, Jennie would not have done well in a strange city alone and far away from her parents. When David was discharged and his in-laws offered, with Jennie obviously wanting to stay, he agreed. This way everyone won. David and Jennie needed the parents' economic strength those first years, and Agneta and John needed the young couple's bodily strength.

That was ten years ago now, Agneta calculated, and long ago, all had become thoroughly accustomed to the living arrangement. There was no more talk of David and Jennie finding their own place. And David constantly helped Agneta in one way or another over the years.

It was David who came to her that morning with tears in his eyes but a steady voice to tell her that John had passed away in the night. It was David who made the funeral arrangements and David who kept his wife busy baking and cooking for the reception at the house following the funeral. That way, he reasoned, she wouldn't fall apart and cause her mother more pain.

Agneta raised her head looking toward the top of the bureau next to her bed to gaze at the black and white photograph taken the day of John's funeral. Her oldest daughter, Magdalene, practical to a fault and emotionally distant, insisted on having the photograph taken that day when everyone was together. Agneta resisted initially, but Magdalene was not to be denied. She was the oldest girl with only one compliant brother two years her senior. She always ruled the younger children into strict conformity to her way of doing things. When the difficult labor with Jennie put Agneta in bed for months after Jennie's birth, Magdalene smoothly took over her mother's position in the house. The competent and self-possessed child grew into a determined and rigid woman.

The day of her father's funeral, Magdalene argued, "We will have all his children and grandchildren dressed in their best clothes and gathered in the house at one time. When does that happen, Mother?"

Agneta wanted to remind her eldest daughter that they always had Sunday dinners together, though, admittedly, long divested of their Sunday clothes. So, as had become the pattern over the years, Magdalene's argument prevailed.

When Agneta's eyes focused again on the photograph, she saw, sitting in the center of the photograph the face of an old woman with sagging jowls and breasts indistinguishable from her curveless body.

Is that really me, she wondered? That sour-faced, old woman is me? It is no surprise that I can't bear to look in the mirror when Jennie does my hair. I understand now why John's passion died long before he did. His young, vibrant wife with tiny waist and silky breasts became this broken mound of flesh. She stared intently at her own face glaring unhappily out of the photograph. An unsmiling, fierce-looking face. The face of a woman who could not be comforted. How can there be any comfort for my guilt, for the cold denials of our bed, for the loneliness I feel so keenly now in his absence, for the dreams, the dreams that will not leave me, she concluded, sighing within and without.

Her husband never reproached her and endured her rejections year after year after the early miscarriages, the births of each of their children. It was hard for her to imagine all those years going by. All those freezing winter nights he came to bed weary from the cold rooms below where he had been tending the books and stoking the fires before he went to bed. They shared that old walnut bed, his mother's gift, the only thing she had been able to give them from her native Germany. The only gift her heartless, violent husband ever allowed her to give her oldest son.

John's mother told me how he and his brothers would step in between their parents to take the blows their father meant for his mother, Agneta recalled. How John did it the first time when he was only twelve. His mother cried in her sorrow, heavy with her own guilt, when she told me the stories of abuse and John's heroic sacrifices. John should be deified for all his sacrifices. The ones he made for me, included. Agneta looked away from the photograph but not from her memories.

The constant work of keeping a dairy farm running profitably had not been easy, especially through the First World War and the long decade of the Depression. The second war brought economic improvement but emotional debilitation. That war itself was not as hard for them as for so many other families. Their oldest son, Albert, did not go off to war because he was partially crippled in an accident on the milk wagon when he was an adolescent. Their middle son, Joseph, already married to Miriam, seemed unfazed by his two years in Europe. But, the youngest, Jacob, could now barely manage his small herd of dairy cattle, his ever increasing family, his overwhelmed wife, and his own nightmares. She knew many families, even in their small community whose sons had not returned at all from that second war.

Jennie came bustling in with late afternoon coffee and the daily newspaper, interrupting Agneta's disturbing thoughts, "You all right, Mother? Need to go potty, I mean, to the bathroom?"

"I'm fine." Agneta closed her diary and set it aside a moment before Jennie laid the newspaper down right where the diary had been.

Agneta generally wanted to read the paper before supper and family time around the television. Television being one of Agneta's guilty pleasures. David brought a television home shortly after Jessie was born. He loved new gadgets, and this was the newest. Programming was sparse in the first months, but before long, there were daily soap operas made for the housewives, Friday night fights for the men, Saturday morning cartoons for the kids, and on Sunday nights family favorites like "Disneyland" and "The Ed Sullivan Show" coming into every American living room. Agneta allowed herself one soap opera, the nightly news, and either "Disneyland" or "Ed Sullivan." Sometimes her middle daughter, Dorothea, would come out at lunchtime to watch "The Guiding Light" with her mother and Jennie.

Jennie wasn't really interested in soap operas or television in general. She said it wasted time to no purpose. But, she would sit with her mother and sister to watch this one, fifteen-minute soap. Jennie wouldn't have admitted even to herself that she liked time away from her housewifely chores. She made it seem like a sacrifice. Jennie liked being the family martyr, though she wasn't the only one.

"Jennie," her mother called. "Did you know that Alice and Frank Collins kept Sylvie out until 2:30 in the morning? Is their neighborhood safe? Why must they stay out so late when she babysits?"

"Mother, really, it was New Year's Eve," Jennie's voice was both amused and irritated. She hated her mother's criticisms about anything to do with the children. "Besides, I stayed up until Sylvie came in. After all, they went to Kansas City and then still drove Sylvie home so she could sleep in her own bed."

Agneta knew such pronouncements from her daughter meant the end of any discussion on the subject. But, Agneta was starting to worry about Sylvie's behavior and her parents' blindness to it. Sylvie was fourteen and quite lovely. She also had a beautiful singing voice which she was increasingly asked to display not only in the choir at church but at voice recitals, tea parties downtown, and who knows where. Agneta did not think that that kind of attention was good for a child who already thought pretty well of herself. Sylvie flaunted the preferential treatment her talent had given her and ladied it over the younger ones. She did it in such dramatic and condescending fashion that Agneta wished Jennie and David would be more conscious of its effect on Gerry and Jessie.

Poor Gerry had been blinded in one eye by Sylvie before either was in school. It was an accident, of course, though Agneta was never completely convinced. She didn't think that Sylvie had been nearly contrite enough about her brother's injury. Although Sylvie fawned over him during the first weeks after it happened, she did so with a smirk of importance rather than a frown of contrition. But Gerry was tough otherwise, and his parents never made an invalid of him. School was hard for him in the first couple of years because his injured eye was drifting and making him cross-eyed. The children at school were, naturally, merciless in their torment of him. Jessie could care less about Sylvie's power plays.

Agneta thought that it was Jessie who most resembled Agneta herself. Jessie was extremely bright and inquisitive, the one who endlessly quizzed her grandmother about the ancestors from "the old country." It was Jessie who played cards with her grandmother, who sat with Agneta for long periods of time while reading or drawing. Jessie explored the world around her and thought about everything deeply. Jennie was constantly pulling Jessie out of the gigantic old elm tree that spread its shade over the children's playhouse. Jessie protesting that she was thinking and singing. Jennie postulating Jessie's imminent demise if she fell from the tall tree. No fear in that one, Agneta mused.

"Think of the Devil," Agneta cried as Jessie came flying into the room from the front door.

"Grammah," Jessie shrieked, "I rode Blue so fast just now and slid off her back end, and, look, look at my britches, Grammah." Jessie gesticulated wildly at her rear end as Agneta exclaimed appropriately over the feat and the fall. But Agneta heard Jennie before she saw her.

"What happened now, Jessie Anne Chapman?" her mother's anguish was real though unnecessary.

"Mama, I rode fast on Blue, fast as the wind goes, and then, whoop! I was off her bottom and on mine," her own verbal play delighted Jessie who continued talking excitedly as her mother steered her into the bathroom for a scrape and bruise check.

Late last summer, Agneta heard Jennie scolding Jessie for breaking rocks on the front porch. Apparently, Jessie collected a pile of rocks from the road and the fields, then found her dad's hammer, and proceeded to wield it with her two tiny hands, smashing the rocks all over the porch. Jessie protested that she wanted to know what was inside, but Jennie's practical sensibilities could not comprehend such inquiry. To Jennie's credit, she had curtailed her harangue relatively quickly and allowed Jessie to continue so long as Jessie cleaned up thoroughly when she finally finished. No loose ends for Jennie. No remaining puzzles.

Agneta smiled and leaned back onto the cane weaving of her wheelchair. To be able to go outside again and see my granddaughter riding and whooping and falling and laughing and cracking rocks apart on the porch. That would be something, she mused.

Agneta used to watch her own children's outdoor games from the big kitchen windows whenever she could steal a few minutes from the constant baking, canning, cooking, and cleaning that went on there. Of course, they never knew she smiled and frowned and delighted in their shenanigans, when those were benign. She never let them see her softness, her loving nature. John saw it, falling in love with the Swedish beauty at first sight.

A community dance at the turn of the century brought all the young people in town together. John was one of the handsome sons of the German dairyman at the end of the old Winchester Road. He and his equally well-wrought brothers dominated any group they were in. Not with overbearing personalities but with their smiling playfulness and acute intelligence, as well as their good looks. The three of them were crowd pleasers wherever they went, John, the eldest, slightly more serious than his younger brothers. These tall, dark-haired young men stood in the center of a group of young men. The young ladies (as their mothers considered them) hovering on the margins trying to catch the young men's eyes without being too bold about it. Then John saw Agneta.

John couldn't speak or move for a few seconds when he saw a beautiful vision walking in with two young men protectively flanking her. Her hair was wound up in the newest fashion with two silver combs adorning each wave above her temples. The hair itself was an unimaginably beautiful shade between clover honey and well-creamed coffee. John was marveling over it when she turned, and her sea blue eyes hit him head on. He literally swayed on the spot. His younger brother, Arthur, the joker of the trio, caught a glimpse of his older brother's face as John swayed toward him. The joke about the beer they'd drunk earlier died on his lips.

"John. What's wrong with you? Are you ill?" Arthur's anxiety was barely held in check since he adored John who had constantly protected him from their brutal father.

"No, no, I'm fine. Look at…Her." John didn't need to point. Arthur just followed his brother's nearly stupefied gaze.

"I see." Arthur appreciated her carefully as he watched his brother's bewitched face.

"I know one of those fellows with her," Arthur said.

"Please let them be her brothers," John pleaded as he took his first steps toward the group.

Agneta would never forget when he first approached her and her brothers. He was so handsome. She kept her eyes lowered as her mother had taught her while her brothers closed in. But, Bror recognized Arthur and slapped him on the back in proper masculine friendship.

She couldn't remember exactly how John managed to get the first dance or the second, before she demurely declined any more dancing. Two dances with one partner was a near engagement in her family. She must be careful that her brothers make no bad report to their mother.

A year later, she was married to the handsome German. They moved to a neighboring state so he could have his own farm, but, two miscarriages later, she longed for home, to be near her mother, her father having died the previous fall after being struck by a street car.

Agneta's father had pampered her lavishly during her girlhood, carrying her to school in the snow so she would not get her feet wet. But he was an alcoholic, and his drunken harangues at her mother and brothers terrified her. She made a pact with herself that, if she married at all, she would never marry a man who drank liquor. When John proposed, she contracted a promise. He would never touch a drop of alcohol again. He loved her and wanted her so thoroughly by then that he would have agreed to any demand she made of him. He never drank alcohol again. Agneta knew he had kept his promise about that as with every other he had made her. He said that he would work hard and keep her and their children always comfortable. He had done so. She never wanted for anything. He laid out her vegetable garden and traded his milk, butter, eggs, even his brother Arthur's handmade ice cream, in exchange for beef from other farmers. John raised pigs, too, and, after keeping some for his family, traded pork as needed during lean, but not empty, years. John gave her strength during the tragedy of their eldest son's crippling accident even as she refused to show signs of grief. Albert's accident was worse than anything else they had faced together.

The snow had fallen heavily that February night. The temperature wasn't frigid but cold enough that large flakes piled up with a biting north wind drifting the snow. The boys, as usual, went out before first light to harness the great draught horses to the milk wagon. The younger boys, Joseph and Jacob, would stay behind to finish the milking while their father and Albert made the rounds. Albert was in the back with the milk to keep the glass bottles steady in their boxes and the ten-gallon cans in place. The roads were slick that morning as the snow melted and refroze into packed ice. The last turn before they could head home was a sharp one down the Myers' narrow lane. They always made that turn carefully even under the best conditions as the wagon barely squeezed down the lane. In the winter darkness and the piled and drifting snow, John had miscalculated by half a foot. The wagon tipped over, and Albert was thrown down, two full milk cans hitting him squarely in the middle of his back. Though his father rushed to him, covered him with his jacket, and ran to the Myers', who had a phone, the doctor couldn't do much more than put Albert to bed with hot compresses on his back. Albert eventually walked again but with a lifelong limp and bent back.

Agneta knew that John had done all he could. She tried to comfort him as well as their son. But she could not break the habit of her own mother's rigid coldness, to be understood as practicality. Agneta could only intone the hollow, religious platitudes that she had inherited: "Thank God that our son is alive. God knows what is best. God has a reason, a purpose for everyone." Cold comfort to the virile young man lying twisted in his bed or to his guilt-stricken, adoring father. Twenty years later, her husband dead and her son still bent and in constant pain, Agneta's wheelchair felt deserved, her punishment. But, from God, or from her own inability to break from her mother's training and example, she would not allow herself to speculate.

"Hello, friend Agneta, how are you?" Lost in her memories, she hadn't heard their longtime friend, Warren Jones, come in. His visits since John died had become more frequent even as his own wife's health prevented her from always accompanying him, or so he said. Fanny still jealous of Agneta's having so many children. Warren and John had been best friends, and their wives had managed to tolerate each other for their husbands' friendship. Warren had a soft spot for Agneta whose beauty and intelligence he had always admired without coveting.

"Warren, I didn't know you were coming today. I must look a fright," she reached up instinctively to push the thick waves that no longer crowned her head. Her hands dropped slowly without completing the movement.

"I was just out getting Fanny a new ring from your brother's shop and thought I'd stop by for a minute to say 'hello'. How are you on this cold January afternoon?" Warren settled himself in a chair at the table next to Agneta. He was the happiest man she knew. His dark hair now silver and his body a bit shorter than it had been, he still had the kindest, most cheerful face. He loved the children, all children. Jessie was a particular favorite. He often teased Agneta that Jessie would become a brighter and better Agneta, if that was possible. Agneta would frown, secretly pleased.

"I'm alright, I guess. No new aches or pains at least, eh?" Agneta shifted in her chair feeling the confinement more than ever with Warren arriving in the midst of her reflections.

They visited about nothing in particular for a little while before Warren rose to take his leave. Jennie offered them coffee and a slice of pie, but Warren must get back to Fanny with his surprise present for her. She possessed more diamonds than anyone Agneta knew. They were all he could offer in place of the children they both had longed for.

Warren's visit and the increasing darkness returned Agneta to early memories. But she couldn't reflect long. Ah, soon, Jennie will bring supper, she thought. We'll watch the evening news on the television, and I will go to bed. To my dreams.

Jennie's careful routine for her mother's bedtime ablutions only took fifteen minutes to complete. Both of them were tired tonight after having visitors. For Jennie, it was the strain of the competing feelings visitors always gave her. Delight at everyone's New Year's greetings, but impatience at the consequent clean-up after each visit. For Agneta, the tiredness came from struggling with her desire to be alone with her thoughts while carrying on conversations with her visitors, even Warren. But now Agneta was in bed and her light was out.

She could barely move her own body anymore to turn herself in bed or to shift her position in her wheelchair during the day. But tonight she lay immobilized by her thoughts.

Why do I feel so blue? My family attentive, a good house around us, kind friends still coming round, my books and crosswords, my crocheting. Maybe I just cannot feel comfort at 74. Frowning, she realized that she could clearly recall the comfort of 19.

Agneta drifted into sleep. She seemed to be at a dance, an engagement party—Warren and Fanny's? Her own? She couldn't see clearly. The strains of a waltz lured couples onto the dance floor where they spun and whirled in blurred sepia tones. Agneta felt John's arm encircle her waist as her hand nestled into his. They turned to take the first step together, but she was suddenly alone on an empty dance floor, the music silenced by her own erratic breathing.

Alexander Bain

The Grey Cairns of Camster. Monuments, gravestones in a pile for a people who lived and died 5,000 years before this day when Maggie and Clare arrive to explore them. As they approach the long cairn by way of the wooden walkway built to keep the tourists from sinking into the bog, they spot a circle of stone identical to that used for the cairns. Once the women read the Historic Scotland posting about the long cairn and take their time to walk and talk over every inch of it, they pick their way carefully across the boggy ground where no walkway exists to reach the circle. Not included in the informative posting near the long cairn, the circle has no sign of its own.

The circle is not closed either. Carefully and intricately laid stones end at about a three-foot opening. The women are left to their own conjectures about its relationship to the stone burial mounds and its purpose. As they walk to the backside of the circle, they notice flatter stones projecting out at intervals beginning halfway round the closed side of the circle and ending about three to four feet before the opening. Maggie steps up carefully onto one of the projecting stones. Her feet fit easily but without room to spare. Clare does the same a few feet further around.

"This has to be a ritual or ceremonial circle, doesn't it?" Maggie begins her hypothesis.

"What else could it be? It's off some distance away from the long cairn, and the opening faces East, I think. The light of dawn and all that."

"Of course, every good ritual begins at dawn. But, it's not like the sun shines on the circle. It's more often overcast than not, isn't it? What about these stones?" Maggie points to her stone perch and Clare's.

"Torchbearers?" Clare guesses. "Maybe these guys held some symbolic pieces, some ritual objects or something?"

Maggie shrugs, "Maybe. Torches until dawn. Remember the blurb on the sign said that platform of slate coming out of the end of the long cairn was *probably* for ceremonial purposes. Maybe this circle was for the final part of the ceremony, the funeral itself."

"Or the sacrifice?" Clare's skin tingles as she speaks.

"Thank you. That's a lovely image. Especially as that boggy ground right there at the opening is blood red. I think I'm ready to—" Maggie jumps off the stone and immediately bends down to pick something up.

"What?" Clare moves off the perch toward her friend.

"It's just a piece of the stone from this wall. Has to be, as there's no other stone like this lying around on the ground." Maggie turns it over in her hand. "Shall we keep it as a souvenir?"

Clare takes no time to answer, "No. If this was a ritual circle connected to the burial or, worse, a spot for an accompanying sacrifice, we will do well to leave it lay."

"I could just put it back in the wall." Maggie shakes off the chill running down her back. "Oh, come on, it's 2003. These people could have been your ancestors. Surely the constant rain and wind have cleared away any bad vibes from 3,000 B.C.E.!" Even as she feels the goosebumps rising on her arms, Maggie laughingly dismisses the sensation. But her own voice still sounds unsure even to her which makes her more determined to do the opposite of what her feelings are telling her at this moment. "Really, Clare, people must pick up these bits all the time. I'm surprised there's anything left with all the American tourists who must have visited here. You know, we're the souvenir junkies of the world!" She laughs unconvincingly.

Clare shakes her head, "I heard about an Australian tourist who removed some stones from another site. After untold calamities, he mailed it back to Historic Scotland."

"Pfah. Let's get back to your house so I can put this in one of my little treasure baggies." Maggie shivers as the cold March wind gains momentum. She places the stone in her coat pocket along with some rocks gathered earlier on the beach, their first stop of the day.

The two women spend a little more time silently walking around the circle, touching the stones in the wall and the ones set on edge near the top. Like the fences all over northeast Scotland, Maggie thinks.

After that, they start back to the wooden walkway. A few minutes more, and they are back in Clare's car heading toward Wick. As they had been doing repeatedly throughout Maggie's visit, they pull over in Wick to explore a cemetery.

The whole cemetery is built on a hillside, and the slabs, laid nearly on top of each other, make small mesas down the hill in step-like fashion. Maggie jumps out and starts taking pictures as soon as Clare turns off the engine.

"Clare, if the modern church and the old ruined one weren't there, it would look like granite bunk beds rising up the hillside with intermittent miniature tower-like drinking fountains or something. Or, like the flagstone cliffs that *are* the northeast coastline," Maggie declares, angling her camera for another shot of one gravestone in particular—*Alexander Bain - a Kind and Affectionate Husband.*

"Do you know anything about fish curers in Pulteney?" Maggie turns to Clare who is bent down reading a different stone.

"A little, yes. Fish curers did just that. They took the fishermen's catch of the day and salt-cured the fish to sell, especially to ships in port needing provisions for long journeys. Here's another one—Peter Sutherland fish-Curer, Pulteney."

Maggie moves to stand beside Clare. "And beside him, another Sutherland of Pulteney. Next to him is Elizabath Rushall, Spouse to John Sinclair Smith. Look how the lettering on her slab is etched around the outside of the granite stone, with the inner rectangle bearing the inscription at the head." Maggie peers down and reads *departed this life February 1680.*

The two women step along slowly through all the slabs, Maggie taking photo after photo. After some time, Maggie turns toward the River Wick and begins walking the gravestones like steps down the hillside. Clare follows and reminds Maggie which direction to look first before crossing the street.

Maggie takes several shots up and down river while Clare consults the time on her watch. "We should head out. You wanted to stop by my folks to say good-bye, didn't you?"

"Yes, of course. I'm ready to go."

Her holiday in Scotland with Clare over, Maggie is on her way home to Seattle. The flight is pretty uneventful even though the old DC-10 bumps and rattles for the entire 11 hours from Gatwick to SeaTac.

When she arrives, Maggie feels that manic edge that only long hours on planes can give. As happy to be home again as she had been to leave ten days before, the travel and sightseeing stress seems good compared to the emotional miasma it displaced. Maggie had sorely needed a change of scene. She knows she should be more careful about contributing to her jet lag but falls into bed as soon as she sets her suitcase down.

Three torches held high off the ground look like candles burning on a shelf in a dark room flickering, moving; the sun rising behind thick clouds, the candles becoming three dark-clad figures holding torches around a circle of stone. Faraway, a single-file line of bodies moves toward the circle—a woman, naked, painted, leading them. Her body blue, ancient woad stain covering her, only a circle of light remaining atop her shoulders. Chanting all around. Where is it coming from? People in animal skins, or animals? Red and black fur, following the blue woman, the chanting growing louder as she steps into the opening of the circle, the man/animal inside beckoning her, the chanting rising and falling until becoming a low, bleating sound like a cat cornering a bird. The others surrounding the circle, bleating, the painted woman inside swaying to the rhythm of the sound louder, more dissonant, bleating, grunting-

Maggie wakes up, head aching, breath shallow, flesh prickling. She lies still until her breathing becomes more normal. Then she reaches out for her oldest cat who always shares her bed.

"Emmy? Emmy? Where are you?" Maggie feels panicky again and bolts up and out of her bed. The old cat sits on the floor near the door as if waiting for something. "Emmy, don't scare me like that. What are you doing?" The cat swirls its tail and steps toward Maggie who scoops her up.

"That was some dream. What the hell was…oh, yeah, jet lag along with some chocolate whatevers from the plane that I ate right before I fell into bed. What time is it?" She struggles a bit to get her bearings and finally locates her clock.

It's 5AM and Maggie's body, still on UK time, struggles with her dream to keep her awake. She puts the kettle on and prepares the teapot. But Maggie can't shake the dream that keeps her head throbbing, lightly, but persistently. The whistling kettle and strong black tea with a little sugar finally displace the sounds in her head.

"It's nearly 1 PM in Scotland. Clare should be at home." Maggie reaches for the phone and dials.

"Clare. Hi."

"Maggie? Everything okay? It's early there!"

"Yea, a bit. 5ish."

"You don't usually get up at five in the morning. What's the matter?"

"Nothing. Nothing. I just woke up. You know, jet lag." Maggie laughs it off.

"I'm about to run to the shops. Can I call you back in a couple of hours?"

"Yeah. No problem. Just felt like a chat. Call me later." Maggie hangs up and the nagging pain in her head returns. She closes her eyes and leans back against the chair. Her younger cat jumps in her lap, and the therapy begins.

Cats never waste a day or feel unfocused or irresponsible. But Maggie does. Four days later, lying now on her living room floor, covered with evasion, irresponsibility, and, of course, her two cats.

She had quit her day job, as she always called it. Cashed in her savings and planned to spend the next six months getting a solid start to a novel. She decided to stop blaming her lack of energy and her writing block on the day job and to give herself no excuses for the next six months. At the end of that time, a new job would be waiting for her, leaving her precious little time for her own writing. So, here she was on the fifteenth day of her six-month plan with nothing to show but Scottish souvenirs, books, and pictures scattered on her work table. And a very clean house.

Maybe I don't have it in me after all, she thought, as she lay staring at the ceiling. What a crappy paint job; they didn't even finish it. That wouldn't take much paint, or time…okay, yet another near-distraction. Avoided. Avoidance. Ah, yes, the Queen of Avoidance. That's me. And, maybe, there is no novel in me. A story, perhaps? Oh, well, time to feed the critters before they attack.

She sits up and cuddles her old cat who never budges voluntarily from a comfortable spot except for food or when a thrashing Maggie dislodges her from the bed. As Maggie moves toward the kitchen, the other cat gets into position. Maggie portions out the food, crushing Chinese herbs for Emmy's rheumatic joints. She thinks about Alexander Bain's headstone in Wick.

Alexander Bain had spent his life in Pulteney near Wick.

Or maybe, Pulteney was Wick before Wick was Wick. No, Wick's been Wick a very long time. One source says that a Pulteneytown was built in 1786 as a "twin burgh alongside Wick." But that's after Alexander's time. And, after the dates for Pulteney folk in the graveyard.

He knew that his life had been no better or worse than any of his neighbors or friends. They had all lost so many that they loved, their children, their parents, their wives and still so much pain.

Maggie voices her questions aloud, "How? How did he lose everyone? Fever of some kind, plague, infant mortality, murder, accidents? The primary bubonic plague years in England in the seventeenth century were 1603, 1625, and 1665—the worst one. But what about northeast Scotland? No source for that yet. Well, I know I need to go back to the library. Use the Internet, maybe get an e-mail correspondence going with a local historian in Wick. Write that down or you'll forget it."

The cats start digging in as she sets the bowls in front of them. My own primary and secondary collection is too early, she thinks, as she distributes the bowls. And, of course, excludes any meaty sources like wills or coroner's rolls or other local archives. Oh, ships' records, customs records? Write it down. If I set him in the fourteenth or fifteenth century, I can draw on research I started in grad school and recreate the quotidian existence of an ordinary life. Lots of good work out there now for these centuries. But, I can't get those gravestones out of my head.

According to Clare and other locals, that was the only typical March day during the time I was there. All-consuming grey, with that deep, damp chill and, of course, the ever-present, vigorous wind from the sea. The pathetically sparse scribblings in my little notebook only comment "Very cold and misty - much could not be seen." That still seems to be the case, Maggie considers.

She shakes her head and walks over to her work table where she has laid out the few photos from that day along with her notes and the first set of sources.

Alexander Bain, a Kind and Affectionate Husband.

I wish the inscription was clearer in the photo. Why didn't I write everything down when I was standing over his gravestone? Or at least brush all the leaves and other debris from it before I took the picture.

Because you left your bag in the car as it was such a novelty to be able to leave your valuables in an unlocked car and go meandering around. And because you already felt like you were trespassing by stomping around from slab to slab, Maggie chides herself.

And had Clare found Peter Sutherland, a Fish-Curer from Pulteney and beside him another Sutherland and the woman, Elizabath Rushall, who was the wife of, what's his name? Oh, yes—here's the photo—John Sinclair Smith. There's a bit more I also can't read here etched in large, capital letters around the outside of the rectangular stone. And that inner stone giving the month and year of her death, February 1680. What does IS EB stand for at the end of that dating? I need to consult a specialist in gravestone studies. Maybe the ethnoarchaeologist whose article I read last week. Maggie reaches for her pen and writes a note about the article "*Archaeology*, pet cemetery in SF."

"Get out of his dish, Miss. You are too fat to have yours and his, too." She picks up Emmy and cradles her like a baby, carrying her into the bedroom to settle in a favorite spot.

As she turns back toward the door, Maggie spies the stack of movies lined up 'just to have something to watch for a break' that she was watching before she left for Scotland—at least one a day, sometimes two. Second time through, at least, she thought. If I want my savings to last six months, I can make a case for not renting any videos with all these damn tapes. I need to put them away and forget that I have *any*, if I'm to get on with my writing.

She picks up the stack and sets the lot in the empty space on the closet shelves with the rest of her video collection. So many taped during her grad school days. The four months that she was writing the stories for her final collection alone, Maggie managed an elaborate system of selecting, setting up the VCR for taping, changing tapes, labeling and storing. For anyone else, it would have been a full-time job. But, somehow, Maggie Kline was able to tape scores of movies while starting and then ending a relationship as well as writing a collection of short stories that won the graduate prize that year. Thirteen years, three jobs, three states, one collection of short stories, and no relationships later, 500 movies sat on those shelves. There had been much to avoid.

Maggie rounds up the cat dishes and keeps up her musings about Alexander Bain, speaking to her cats as audience, "Carved into the 'feet' of Elizabath Rushall's stone slab, the skull and crossbones with *Memento Mori*—remember that you must die—who could forget in a time when the average life expectancy in Scotland was about 30. Above the reminder, a Latin cross and a crown. The 'death's head,' a common symbol of *memento mori*. The first ones I saw in Scotland triggered a vague recollection of its use as a warning in ancient Rome anyway.

She sits down at her table, scans the pictures, takes more notes, and then writes, Alexander Bain, born in Pulteney 1662; fish-curer's apprentice, age 12; fish-curer in his own right, age 20; married Elizabath Sutherland 1682; first child, Mary Elizabath born 1683; second child Alexander Kenneth born 1685, died 1687; third child, Peter John born 1690, died 1697 along with his mother, Elizabath.

"O.K., kitties, I stole Elizabath Rushall's first name for Alexander Bain's wife. A common given name for girls at that time anyway," she justifies as Emmy opens one sleepy eye. But did the plague have another go in 1697 in Scotland, she wonders to herself? The last reference I found to it was in 1645 around Edinburgh. Too far south? How did two survive while all others were lost?

That question had troubled Maggie again and again as she wandered through graveyards in Caithness and Sutherland.

The later eighteenth- and early nineteenth-century stones were the most informative, of course. Whole families listed on one stone. Many dying as children, young women, probably in childbirth, as the ages indicate. Men dying in their 20s, 30s, 40s, then one old man or woman in the family whose name is carved at the last because he or she lived into their 80s. Even one or two over the age of one hundred. The Anglo-Saxons had a word for that—*wyrd*. Fate.

Fortune's wheel? Shit happens, she mused. And, how do I get them literate? He could have learned to read and write for the benefit of his trade, having been taught by his master, Elizabath's father, whom I will call Peter Sutherland. But what about the girl, his daughter, Mary? I suppose her mother might have taught her as her father had done for Elizabath. By the late seventeenth century, there were schools for boys and girls, but the curriculum was totally gendered. Don't teach girls what they need to function independently. Teach them only what will make them a good wife. But, there were girls being taught. What did that article say? Here it is: "Discrimination against females in this period is visible both in the curriculum which girls were taught in their access to educational resources and in their attainment of reading and writing skills." Classic. Confine them to the home, educate them only enough to get better work out of them in the domestic realm. What else does he say? "Cultural values among the Scottish population dictated that girls' learning be limited to practical skills…for their approved role in society…[one contemporary wrote that girls] are taught what their parents or guardians judge as necessary or useful for them to learn…either to improve the natural attractions of their person, or to form their mind to reserve, to modesty, to chastity, and to economy." Of course, he was talking about the middle class, not the lower class to which Mary Bain would belong. What of them? "For the lower classes the practical skills taught to girls would enable them to be productive partners in marriage." But he also notes that there were men, fathers, who thought girls' educations should be more than "decorative." Why wouldn't Elizabath's father *and* Alexander Bain, as her husband and the father of Mary, be one of those more enlightened men? Maybe I'm complicating this when it doesn't need to be, but I want it to be historically accurate and still interesting.

Alexander Bain put his hand gently on his daughter's head. Her face turning up to his showed the same pain, but different questions. Alexander looked back at the stone slab. ELIZABATH SUTHERLAND, BELOVED WIFE OF ALEXANDER BAIN AND DEVOTED MOTHER LIES HERE WITH HER PRECIOUS SONS ALEXANDER AND PETER The carving had been done well. He was satisfied. Elizabath would be. She had always wanted a stone carved for her first son, but money had been short then. Now, fishing had been good for years, while the export of his cured fish rose and fell with the political bickering between the monarchy settled so far south and its relations all over Europe and now the Colonies. But even if he had had to beg the money, he would have, for this, for her. Now what would they do?

Maggie bursts out, "That's the problem isn't it! Now, what? What's the point? Where would a late seventeenth-century Scottish fish-curer and his daughter go after they walk out of that graveyard?"

Her thoughts continue her argument. "It's too early and too far north for Thomas Gray to elegize them and his poem was limited largely to praising himself. What would he say about fish-curers and their wives and children? His country churchyard was filled with farmers and, apparently, only had men in it. "Some village-Hampden, some mute, Milton, some Cromwell." I always wondered which Cromwell he was referencing there, both of them being suspect, self-servers. Well, it was (and is) a man's world especially for someone of Gray's class and persuasion. Oh, well. That was 1750s' England not 1690s' Scotland." Suddenly, two cats come flying across her desk breaking Maggie's train of thought.

"Hey, you two." Maggie starts to get out of her chair but sits right back down. Alexander Bain wouldn't yet be silenced.

No wonder I thought about Thomas Gray. Everything I picked up the other day, quoted the "Elegy." Austen, *Archaeology*, an 1891 issue of *Notes and Queries*. Strange. Such vastly different sources to quote the same eighteenth-century English poet. The phone rings and startles her out of her reverie.

"Hi, Clare. Thanks for calling back. Any more gossip about that weird guy down the street? Good. No news ,as they say. Yes, I did do some scribbling today. Not much, just some notes. I think I did. Remember the Thomas Gray day I told you about? I was just thinking about it again. I had been ignoring the Alexander Bain idea, but, after our conversation, I finally started to believe that Thomas Gray's 'Elegy' being quoted at me from all sides was, indeed, a sign. So, I reread the poem—more than once. No, not at first. No great revelation anyway.

The only thing was the graveyard connection. You know, the poor folk with no one to tell their stories, no great deeds to relate. Maybe that's it. Sure. Most people don't perform great deeds except, of course, the greatest one of all—getting through a life. But, who will want to read a book about that? Yes, I know, there's always something extraordinary in an ordinary-seeming life, in fiction at least. Look at Eudora Welty's stories. Ordinary people. You're right. No one's life is devoid of interest. There's always some perversity, some crime to soul or body or both, unacknowledged, undetected or unpunished. Maybe I'm too worried about my audience when this story is chomping at the bit to be told. O.K., I promise. I'll just write. I know. It does seem to want to be written. But, what if I'm not the writer? Sorry, writer's angst. So, tell me what's going on with you and your sister?"

They continue talking about everything but Alexander Bain for an hour. Yet, when Maggie hangs up the phone, Alexander is still there.

His dark hair and fair skin matched his daughter's in tone and shade. Yet, his grey eyes were a pale reflection of her deep blue ones. Alexander Bain put his arm around his daughter and slowly steered her and himself down the hill and out of the graveyard. They crossed the path that followed the River Wick and paused.

Well, that's what *I* did anyway. I walked down the hill over the stone wall and stared at the river and back at the graveyard. The river was only a slightly darker version of the sky but moving swiftly with the wind and the current. The three arches of the bridge beyond were another shade darker, still grey. Looking down the river toward the bridge and the town or upriver toward Haster and Watten, everything seemed grey and marvelous. With the mist, a Monet in grey. Rewrite.

His dark hair and fair skin matched his daughter's in tone and shade. Yet, his grey eyes were a pale reflection of her deep, blue ones. A stark contrast to the shades of grey that surrounded them in the March mist. Alexander Bain put his arm around his daughter and slowly steered her and himself down the hill and out of the graveyard. They crossed the path that followed the River Wick and paused.

Yet, standing in the cemetery itself, the grey of its stones, of the old ruin of a chapel, of the still barren trees was diffused by the moss, growing everywhere on the stones, the chapel, the trees. Grey again took over the stone wall that marked the church's and the cemetery's boundaries. A buffer between the dead and the living. But touching the stone wall and spreading out toward the road were the dark green-leaves and yellow-heads of jonquils that grew there. Still, that has to be a relatively recent addition. The stone wall, too, is old but not there in Bain's day. Then the grey of the pavement of the highway, was it the same shade of dirt or gravel of the narrow river path in the late seventeenth century? When I crossed the pavement, its grey gave way to the pale green of the grass on the riverbank where I had stood staring at the river before I turned from the other stone wall along the river and crossed the Safeway parking lot. I bought a soda and some packaged crackers to get me through to lunch in Lybster. But Alexander and Mary had no Safeway—only the narrow path—probably just as covered with dead leaves and broken sticks as the cemetery was now where I have left Alexander and Mary standing.

Mary pulled the hood of her thick wool cloak over her head and gathered the cloak itself tight around her as she turned from the river and headed down the path toward Pulteney. Her movement brought Alexander back to her, but as he turned to join her, he was struck by her walk, her form. At 14, so like her mother's. Would the pain ever stop? But, no he didn't want it to stop. Who should feel it but him? Elizabath and little Peter couldn't feel anything now. And, they were guiltless.

Where did that come from, Maggie wondered? What is Alexander hiding? There's no plague or disease here. Accident then? A skiff or coracle capsized in the river? Why would those two be out alone in it? Were they alone? Who might have been with them? Alexander?

As Alexander and Mary walked slowly toward home, the wind-whipped river was a constant reminder. It was always incredibly misty in the late winter afternoons. That day had been no different.

The dark grey of the sky melted into the darker grey of the river but no foreboding gripped them as Alexander, Elizabath, and little Peter climbed into the skiff. Mary had stayed at the shop to meet her friend, Annie Sinclair.

Pretty melodramatic, but life is like that, at least for trauma and loss, Maggie considers. The six weeks that Dad was in the hospital, the day he died all fade to grey in the bedroom where he suffered and died. I know the sun was shining outside all day because the hospice worker who kept me on the phone for ten minutes that morning said something like, "it's a beautiful day to die," or some crap like that. But, my father didn't want to die any more than Elizabath. The weather is always grey on such a day.

The weather had been just short of a storm all day, but nothing extraordinary for March. Grey. Damp. Cold. With a strong wind. But little Peter had wanted to see the ship in port in Wick. Bound for the Colonies—full of slaves. Good for business but, truly, not for the soul. But, Peter wanted so badly to see it. Elizabath came to watch over us both, I suppose. It wouldn't be a long or difficult trip for three in a skiff. What went wrong?

Good question, Alexander, Maggie thinks. How could someone like

Alexander not be able to steer a damn boat down a river, even a choppy one? Maggie keeps staring at the picture of the river, looking down toward Wick proper. She tries to imagine the stone bridge gone; it wouldn't have been there for Alexander. But, the shades of grey are right. More mist, maybe for their journey, more wind, if that's even possible. For me, it was the dampest, windiest day and the greyest. Maybe by late afternoon the clouds were as low as when I was there. By the time we got to Westerdale in the late afternoon that day, it was hard to see very far. As the dark set in on their way back, maybe—

Little Peter couldn't sit still or stop talking on the way back from the ship. He was full of its billowing sails and huge masts, of the crew that revolted Elizabath by their filth and by their callousness for the cargo they carried. With one eye on her son, she sat wondering about their complicity in selling their cured fish to such people. Suddenly, the boat lurched from side to side as Peter tried to move from Elizabath to his father at the other end of the skiff. Elizabath and Alexander both started toward him at the same moment, and the boat capsized plunging them headlong into the cold, grey river. Alexander hit the water but instantly righted himself. His eyes searched for the other two as the current took the boat out of his reach. He saw their heads bobbing in the water just a few feet from him but in two different directions. He went for the one closest to him. It was Elizabath. She could swim well enough but was being pulled down by something. She got her head above water again and screamed for him to get the boy. Alexander turned immediately toward where Peter's head had been seconds before. It was gone. "Peter!" he screamed. He saw Peter thrashing about in the direction of the boat, trying to keep his head up. Alexander swam toward the boy. He grabbed him a few seconds later. He turned in the water with Peter tucked under one arm but still thrashing. He tried to calm him with his voice and still move toward Elizabath. But he couldn't see her anymore. His head turned in all directions, but she wasn't there. The night kept falling around him, and the water suddenly felt unbearably cold. He knew he had to get his son to shore. But Elizabath! He felt confused and then a thought gave him energy and hope as he swam with the boy toward the riverbank. She would be there waiting. She had always been a strong swimmer. Although her mother had objected to her getting in the water with the boys, her father had insisted that she needed to know how to swim. Ridiculous to live on the water and not be able to swim—boy or girl. The hope surged through Alexander and helped him get Peter swiftly to shore. He pulled the boy up onto the bank and turned him over to drain out any water in his head and chest. Peter coughed and sputtered then sat up. "Mother!" he cried. "Hush, boy, she's right here." Alexander kneeling now at his side, wrapped one arm around the boy and threw his head from side to side as he twisted his body to see her. But she wasn't there. He told the boy to stay where he was, and then Alexander dove back into the icy river. Night descended and, with the cold water, blurred Alexander's vision as he swam to where he thought she had been. He dove under the white-capped surface and tried to open his eyes in the murky water. He couldn't. He lashed out with his arms and went deeper. He came back to the surface for air and another look across the choppy waters. Nothing there. Just wind and water. Panic rose in his throat and choked him as he gasped for air after another dive. "Elizabath!" he heard himself scream as if from far away. The cold crawled up his limbs, his chest, his head.

I hate predictability. We know they're going to end up in the water as soon as we see the boat. But, maybe—

Alexander came to, shivering, covered with a blanket and being carried into a house. Elizabath and Peter sat near the fire already. Am I dreaming or in heaven? God let this be real, he thought. "Alexander!" Elizabath jumped up and rushed toward her husband as the men eased him onto a stool next to his son's. The joy was overwhelming but short-lived.

Maggie's return to the moment comes with a clash and clatter. One of her cats is playing soccer with a stainless steel bowl in the kitchen sink.

"Stop it, Peabody! God, you're timing is always impossible. Sleeping, writing, relaxing is not allowed, eh? Cut it out." She gets up and puts the bowl in the dishwasher as the offending cat heads at high speed for another bit of mischief with his sibling. "Good, you two chase each other up and down the hallway but stay out of things!"

Maggie sits down again and stares at what she's been writing.

The joy was overwhelming but short-lived. A week later both Peter and Elizabath were dead. The surgeon from Wick had called it an infectious fever caused by the river water they had swallowed. But, why, then didn't I die, too? Alexander couldn't stop punishing himself. The pain of his daughter, her distress, didn't reach him at first. Only when they buried Elizabath and Peter next to his firstborn son, did Alexander realize he still had Mary.

Nah. Dying of an infectious fever, maybe. But lose the boat bit. Let's go back to where he notices that Mary is starting to resemble her mother. O.K., cut that bit about pain and guilt, lose the boating accident, rescue, and subsequent death. Let's see—

Mary pulled the hood of her thick wool cloak over her head and gathered the cloak itself tight around her as she turned from the river and headed down the path toward Pulteney. Her movement brought Alexander back to her, but as he turned to join her, he was struck by her walk, her form. At 14, so like her mother's. Would the pain ever stop? Not for the living. As Alexander and Mary walked slowly toward home, the wind whipped up whitecaps on the surface of the river. The dark grey of the sky became the darker grey of the river. They continued in silence until they were in their cottage with a fire just starting to shed light on the interior and their faces. Numbed by grief, wind, and cold, father and daughter sat in the emptiness musing to themselves for some time before Mary spoke. "Can we leave here?" The echo of his own thoughts startled him.

Why leave, she wonders? Why would they leave where they had been all their lives, where their loved ones were buried, where they had a decent business? Why stay where everything reminded them of their loss? Could Alexander and Mary find their way on board a ship bound for the Isthmus of Panama in 1698 for the ill-fated Darien scheme? Need to read more on that if I can find more. I'm limited in Scottish historical resources here. The Pacific Northwest isn't exactly a hot spot of Scottish settlement.

Maggie starts cutting and pasting, rewriting and revising. Time always escapes her when she's lost in the words and the story. Hours pass before she realizes she needs nourishment. Maggie puts the kettle on and fixes a simple cheese sandwich only half attending to what she is doing. She can't leave Alexander and Mary alone. "No," she says aloud. "It's time to print this out. I have to see it before I add another word or move another sentence around." With the first pages before her, she picks up half of her sandwich and begins to read:

At 35, Alexander Bain of Pulteney had already exceeded the maximum life expectancy of a man living on the northeast coast of Scotland in 1697. He knew it without any future scholars of early modern Europe making the calculations for him. He had lost two sons, his wife, his parents, and most of his nearest relations. Not to mention friends. He was an old man by the reckoning of the day and a damn lucky one at that to have one child of 14 still alive and well. In fact, Mary had hardly had a sick day in her life. Alexander hadn't had any particular inclination to leave the town where he was born or go much farther than the necessary business trips to the nearby royal burgh of Wick. He had apprenticed with his then, future, father-in-law when it was still important to do so. That, of course, was out of fashion today. Young people wanted to get right to running the business. Naturally, those businesses failed after the original master passed on so the young people moved on. From job to job and town to town. Now, would he and Mary move on too?

He put his hand gently on his daughter's head. Her face turning up to his showed the same pain but different questions. Alexander looked back at the stone slab. ELIZABATH SUTHERLAND BELOVED WIFE OF ALEXANDER BAIN AND DEVOTED MOTHER LIES HERE WITH HER PRECIOUS SONS ALEXANDER AND PETER. The carving had been done well. He was satisfied. Elizabath would be. She had always wanted a stone carved for her firstborn son, but money had been too scarce then. Fishing had been good now for years, but the export of his cured fish rose and fell with the political bickering between the monarchy so far south and its relations all over Europe. Now the Colonies were adding business. But even if he had had to beg the money for the carving, he would have. Now what would they do?

Alexander Bain put his arm around his daughter and slowly steered her and himself down the hill and out of the graveyard. His dark hair and fair skin matched his daughter's in tone and shade. Yet, his grey eyes were a pale reflection of her deep, blue ones. A stark contrast to the shades of grey that surrounded them in the March mist. They crossed the path that followed the River Wick and paused.

Mary pulled the hood of her thick, wool cloak over her head and gathered the cloak itself tight around her. Her movement brought Alexander back to her, and they turned from the river and headed down the path toward Pulteney. As Alexander and Mary walked slowly toward home, the wind whipped up whitecaps on the surface of the river. The dark grey of the sky melted into the darker grey of the river. They continued in silence until they were in their cottage with a fire just starting to shed light on the interior and their faces. Numbed by grief, wind, and cold, father and daughter sat in the emptiness musing to themselves for some time before Mary spoke. "Can we leave here?" The echo of his own thoughts startled him.

That's it, Maggie thinks? That's all I have after…how long? Four paragraphs in four days? I leave it alone, come back, write, revise, refine. Four lousy paragraphs. What is the point? I dream about this stuff, but I can't remember the words when I wake up.

Maggie pushes the pages away from her and slowly sips her tea, cold now, but she doesn't notice.

Maybe I need to get rid of Alexander Bain and bring his wife back to life, she posits. Mother and daughter left on their own to find their way. All the men dead. That could be. Women weren't dying in childbed at such high rates as earlier or even later, at least in Scotland. They could have better than the minimal education because there were parents who wanted more for their girls. Her father could have taught her the business as well. But some laws still restricted women's independent activities or tried to do so.

Maggie thumbs through one of the books near her on the table: "Edinburgh burgesses complained [in the early eighteenth century] that women and male unfreemen were setting up shops illegally. Competition from anyone who did not have official burgess privileges to trade within the town was the issue." That was far to the south of Elizabath. Besides, she would be a widow and free. She would have the most legal and economic freedom. "Widows were effectively on a par with men." So, why not Elizabath and Mary standing over the grave that I actually saw—that of Alexander Bain? "Because then the title of the novel couldn't be Alexander Bain, could it?" The high pitch she reaches with this remark sends the cats skittering to the other end of the house.

I can still explore the issues I want to address about women's lives with Mary, Maggie reasons. At 14, she's far from marriageable at least in late seventeenth-century Scotland. One of the historians that I've read indicates that women were, generally, not married until 23-26 years of age. That gives me some time to see the struggles of a single woman even with her father still in the picture. I am curious about Alexander Bain's life and can keep both of these characters at the center without displacing either one too much. It's just such a great name. Start with a great title and—

Maggie's musings are interrupted again by one of her cats. Having to get up to check, she realizes she is tired. Then, she remembers the dream. She has convinced herself that jet lag and weird food choices were the culprits. That way she can put it out of her mind. Until now. Oh, I'm just tired and immersed in Scottish history, she argues. Maybe I should watch some cartoons before I fall asleep.

She rummages through her tapes and finds a very old one of her favorite Warner Brothers' cartoons. "This will take me someplace else for sure," as she speaks she ruffles the soft fur of Emmy's head. Maggie pops the tape into the VCR, goes through her pre-bed ablutions and then settles into bed. About three cartoons in, she begins to nod off. The bulldog has just put the little kitty on his back to fall asleep when Maggie does.

Chanting, more like the hum a house makes when all is suddenly quiet. Soon the hum becomes a deafening roar. Then silence again. No clear images. Like dusk during a heavy rainstorm, things are undulating, moving across her dream-restricted vision. Then she feels a hand, many hands on her legs, her arms, her back, pushing her forward toward a center point in the distance. The scene changes, she sees clearly—the circle, the short, blue people covered in part by red-black shaggy hair, not their own. She's watching and joining all at once. Who's that bleating, then bellowing? His face distorts with sound. Why is he reaching out for me? Must run, get over this wall. The rocks tearing at her flesh, her very, heavy legs, caught by something, pulling her down.

As Maggie tries to leap out of bed, she falls flat on the floor, legs impaled by her bedspread. The pain of hitting the hardwood floor brings her instantly awake.

"Shit!" Maggie howls in pain as the two cats run around frightened by this interruption in their dreamless sleep.

Once she has her bearings, Maggie gets up off the floor and pulls her bedroom door shut to view the damage in the full-length mirror on the back of the door.

"O.K., no major bruises, but is that a big, red bump rising on the side of my head? What is that dream?"

Maggie opens the door and walks down the hall to the living room where all her photos and notes lay strewn across the table. She passes the table, stopping a few feet away at a small shelf protruding from the wall. She lifts a stone from the shelf and turns it in her hand.

"Is it you intruding on my dream life, shackling my creativity? Cursing me?" she frowns at the stone and starts to put it back on the shelf. But then, she has second thoughts.

She holds the stone in one hand and fumbles in one of her desk drawers with the other, finally drawing out a padded envelope about the size of a paperback. Maggie stares at the stone for another minute before placing it inside the envelope. With a black marker, she writes Clare's address on the front of the envelope. Inside with the stone, Maggie slips a folded piece of notepaper on which she has written:

Clare, please take this stone back to the circle at the Grey Cairns, Camster.

Please!

xoxo Maggie.

As she pulls off the light strip of paper covering the adhesive and seals the envelope, Maggie practically shouts, "Tomorrow, you are on your way home! What dreams may come!"

The Friar's Secret Stash

I jumped off the 205 bus at the British Library and walked the little way to King's Cross as quickly as the late afternoon mass of commuters would allow. For the journey to York, I carried my satchel with a few clothes but mostly stuffed with relevant research notebooks and lots of those blue Blackwell bookshop pencils from the shop in Oxford. After an overnight in York, I would catch another train to Northallerton.

According to a variety of travel websites I consulted before this trip, I could pick up a bus for the last few miles of my journey. But I had never been to the English Heritage site of Mount Grace Priory, so I didn't really know the lay of the land at all. In fact, it would be my first trip to York. I couldn't wait to get to that ancient city. I was as excited as I had been at ten years of age, dragging my long-suffering mother to see the little museum I'd created in the old bull shed on my grandparents' farm.

Three hours later, I stepped off the train at York rail station and wandered along the road toward the city centre. I bought a map out of a box for £1 but found that I didn't really need it. Everyone who had alighted from that train was moving like a line of ants toward the sugary Sunday picnic cake that was York Minster.

When we crossed the bridge over the River Ouse, I found myself again school-girlish with excitement. But as I started past the Pizza

Express into the city just across the bridge, the fragrant smell of pizza and pasta highlighted the hours that I had gone without food since morning. My excitement to get to the bed and breakfast and on to the sights struggled with my insistent hunger. As usual, hunger won out, and I went inside the restaurant.

The wine was calming and my favorite Pizza Express dish was as good as expected. The service, on the other hand, was not what I had been used to in London. I laughed at myself for thinking like a Londoner after only a few months' residence. When I finished my food, I continued for a little while to sip my wine and consider in a calmer way why I had left my research in London at this particular moment to spend the weekend, by myself, on the grounds of a late fourteenth-century Carthusian monastery in the midst of the North York Moors.

Besides the obvious fact that my research had actually led me here—Mount Grace being one of hundreds of religious houses destroyed by Henry VIII's minions and subsequent iconoclasts after the Dissolution—this monastery was also one of the most intact monastic ruins from that period. The monks post-Dissolution history was mostly shrouded in mystery. A hint of which I had glimpsed obliquely in one document.

I hadn't been able to unravel that mystery in any of my library or archival searches. Just as I would be certain that I found something and traced a logical path, I'd run into a dead-end. Not unlike the literal dead-ends I encountered in Stafford, dutifully following a map which only led me to one wrong turn after another where I'd end up facing a wall instead of a cross street.

Only two days ago, I decided to stop looking in the archives, arm myself with the new Candace Robb medieval mystery novel, and try to ferret out my real medieval mystery. I hoped for inspiration at least, if not for resolution.

As I walked out of the restaurant, I breathed in the surprisingly warm air of a May day. Sunshine and blue sky abounded just as it did in California this time of year. But, no town or city in California, however quaintly contrived, could match York.

York thrived as a pastiche of ancient and modern, a mixture of human machinations engineered over the centuries. In that at least, York reminded me of Oxford. It was in Oxford where I had first been deflated by the sight of a modern glass box souvenir and ticket cubby abutting the eleventh-century tower at the North Gate. This tower once housed the Bocardo Prison where, in 1556, Thomas Cranmer awaited his execution. In the twenty-first century, tickets were being sold in the modern glass box for entrance into St. Michael's Church and the tower itself. The prison door, behind which Cranmer contemplated his death, stands as an unhinged artifact in the church and tower museum. Medieval-to-modern dissonance intact. After a while though, this collage of time felt as natural as any other human concoction.

I found a pleasant irony in an electronics shop inhabiting the lower floor of a building with the top floor looming out in proper sixteenth-century fashion. That caught my eye as I leaned against the outside of the medieval Saxon Tower enjoying a French *pain aux raisins* and coffee from a little café cart peddling its wares nearby. Of course, I loved the old pubs nestled just inside the medieval wall, especially the Turf Tavern, where I sat with my feet resting on the line of the medieval city wall while finishing the last bell's cider or ale in near medieval darkness. York also was a medieval-to-modern collage.

As I left Pizza Express and walked toward York Minster, I encountered a succession of people dressed in varying degrees of authentic Victorian garb hawking a "ghost walk" down one eerie lane or another.

I picked the older gentleman in long black coat and top hat, his longish silver hair protruding from his hat. His tour would begin at half-eight that night. As I turned back toward the walkway between shops, another illusion caught my eye; a statue of a man-or a man of a statue-on a bicycle, faux basset hound puppy in his basket and dog ears, scarf, hair, and coattails flapping in a breeze that wasn't. Man, dog, and bicycle all painted in a ghastly shade of purple. The only incongruity in the tableau was the rather putrid orange mini-bin which sat on the front right edge of the 'statue's' rectangular pedestal with a hand-printed 'Thank You' on a post-it note sticking out of the mouth of the bin.

Later, I saw the same 'statue' talking to a man on stilts in black eighteenth-century garb with a sign for "Haunted Vaults Tour" on a stick attached to a small carrier holding tour pamphlets. I was in a historians' heaven. Or hell, depending on your sense of humor.

Strolling along the narrow stone street past the 'statue' and his mate, I headed toward the cathedral. My disappointment was immense when I found that I couldn't go in because they were preparing for some kind of special evening concert which included a modern religious service of no interest to me. I contented myself with a photo shoot of the outside taken from every conceivable angle . When I finished, I noticed that the meeting place for my ghost tour later that night would be right across from the front entrance. Finally, I went in search of my B&B.

It sat just outside the medieval loop of York. As I walked away from the bridge and down along the riverwalk toward my hotel, another touristy possibility for the evening stopped me, an after-dark tour of the river from that spot to slightly beyond Bishopthorpe Palace. I couldn't pass that up and would just be able to make it after the ghost tour.

I checked into my B&B but found the path to my room a bit ominous, through winding narrow passages, reminiscent of the medieval city itself, and again with clearly modern features intruding. By the time I found my room, I was feeling a bit isolated. All the rooms along the way were unoccupied. But when I went into the room, it was warm, cozy, and thoroughly modern.

The ensuite had the tiniest jacuzzi tub I'd ever seen, squeezed in with toilet and sink. The bathroom itself was about as small as it could be and still be functional. The ingenuity of the British to use what space they had to the utmost still amazed me. A door on the other side of my room opened into a garden set along the length of the hotel. I made a mental note to come back to York to this hotel when I could spend more than one night.

The garden with its quaint table and two chairs would be great for the reading that relaxed me the most, mysteries set in medieval York, accompanied by my CD compilation of jazz and a perfectly chilled (by the night air) bottle of pinot noir. But at that moment, time was already slipping away. I went back inside, packed my day bag for the afternoon and evening ramblings, and, shouldering my bag, left the B&B to explore the city.

The only sour note of the evening tours was on the riverboat where a pair of obnoxious couples thought everyone else should be interested in hearing their achingly ignorant and insipid conversation. I braved the cold of the upper deck for the full ninety-minute tour to escape them. The delight I had felt in the sights along the river and an inner fury at the morons below managed to warm me for the duration of the trip.

Afterward, I stepped off the boat, moored slightly past the graffiti-laden sign for Dame Judi Dench Walk. My back garden space and my warm bed were but a few steps away.

A hot jacuzzi half-hour frnd a glass of wine put me into bed with Owen Archer. I drifted off just as he was about to discover that a reported accidental death was, in fact, murder.

I woke with a start and a small string of obscenities that I hadn't uttered since I was a fresh-mouthed college student. Was I still dreaming? I flicked the switch for the lamp nearest my head, but it didn't come on. "Alright, this isn't funny, even in a dry, English sort of way," I croaked aloud to the room. What *was* that sound? A high pitched, human…cackle? Do people really cackle? It was too supernatural to believe so I chose not to believe it.

The next sound rent the silence. The chill that went up my spine right over the top of my head couldn't be ignored. I realized the ghost tour I blithely joined the evening before had stirred up more than adrenalin. An unsettling primal response lapped my cells from head to toe.

A dusky ghost tour, a dark riverboat ride, and a murder mystery make a bad thought cocktail before bed. Out the window I could just see the white glow of a face looking up into the lamplight with a rather devilish grin. With my rational mind shaking off sleep, I saw the foolish face of a teenaged boy surrounded by a few wiggling, dancing human forms with spray cans in their hands. Ah, the graffiti painters coming back to add more nonsense to that perfectly lovely sign. Dame Judi Dench deserves better than these youths without a substantive thought among them.

Remembering the empty-headedness of my own youth, I felt suddenly old and crawled back into the warm bed. Back to sleep before I start reminiscing or cringing about my own teenage antics. Owen, where were we? I reached for the novel and located the correct switch for the lamp which lit without a flicker of hesitation.

I awoke earlier than I expected but felt refreshed in spite of my disrupted sleep. Still, Owen Archer's adventures hadn't been very helpful in forestalling bad dreams. No time to muse over fiction when reality demanded movement.

It felt good to be up and able to have breakfast before I needed to catch the 10:15 to Northallerton, the cheapest day single. I'd be there in twenty-three minutes. A breeze.

And it was. Soon I was in the little rail station in Northallerton buying an egg salad sandwich and enquiring about the bus service to Mount Grace Priory.

"Mount Grace Priory?" the clerk seemed puzzled. "Olivia, do you know a Mount Grace Priory?"

"You mean the school, Roger?" Olivia answered from the other side of the small station.

"Do you mean the priory school, Miss?" Roger turned to me with a hopeful smile.

"No," I said gently holding back my surprise at their confusion. "The ruins of the charterhouse of Mount Grace Priory. The English Heritage website said it was about six miles north of Northallerton and that the no. 80 bus would take me there." I looked from Roger to Olivia, with my own hopeful smile.

"No, no. I don't know of any bus like that. Maybe one of the drivers outside can help you." That was clearly Roger's final offer as he went back to putting sandwiches in the cooler.

"Cheers." I didn't really mean it but went on outside with hope fading fast.

Astonishingly, the first cabbie I queried said that he could take me there in no time for a mere £16. I had learned quickly not to do the conversion even in my head, or I would be depressed all the time about the sad state of the American dollar.

Consequently, I hopped into his cab with my satchel and off we went. Joe the Cabbie introduced himself and started talking right away about how he had lived in Northallerton only two months but was liking it so far and was I an American and why was I in Northallerton and who was at the priory school where we were headed.

"Hang on. Sorry. It's not the priory school I'm going to. It's Mount Grace Priory, the monastery ruins six miles north of here?" Please know what I'm talking about.

"Oh. Hmm. Well, let me just stop here a minute and check" which he said and acted upon in the same breath.

We pulled into a petrol station with a store, and I thought it wise to go along to add to Joe's enquiry. There, too, we met with more questions than answers. Two people were happy to offer opinions about where it *might* be. So Joe and I started off again.

The opinions of one of the storekeepers along with my own assertions about the route got us to the A19 in a few more minutes. But before we had moved along the highway less than a mile, Joe was pulling over again. This time to consult with a highway vendor he knew.

It only took a couple of minutes before he was back in the cab with me in my own peculiar shock that the whereabouts of a 600-year-old monastery would be the mystery of the day! But Joe came back happy and full of accurate directions so that five minutes later we were crossing on a narrow connector between the opposing lanes of the A19. As we waited on the connecting path, I saw my no. 80 bus whiz by. I sighed a heavy breath of exasperation as we crossed the lanes to pull onto the more welcoming path.

Any remaining chagrin gave way as we wound down the half-mile drive to Prior's Lodge, the seventeenth-century manor house 'add-on' to the monastery. This would be my home for the next two nights and days. I nearly came out of my seat when we reached the sign: Mount Grace Priory Best Preserved Carthusian Monastery in Britain. One last sarcastic thought crossed my mind as we passed: Best *Hidden* Carthusian Monastery in Britain.

Joe and I parted, delighted with each other at the last. He, because he had information on a destination that was sure to be fruitful for him in the summer months ahead which information he would have over the local cabbies. And I, because I was, at long last, on the grounds once inhabited by the monk who carried *The Book of Margery Kempe* out of the monastery after a residence of nearly one hundred years to be lost to the world for nearly four hundred more. I felt as if I had come home.

Anxiety gone, a very homey need arose indeed. Another sign at the gate had promised a gift shop and toilets, along with the assurance that picnics were welcome. I patted the sandwich, crisps, and Coke in my bag. The necessity of the second item, however, overrode any other thoughts as Joe pulled up and let me out.

York's unseasonable warmth had caused me to leave my wool jacket at the B&B since I would be returning there after the weekend at the monastery. Unfortunately, Mount Grace lay at the edge of the North York Moor where the morning marine layer had already come over the hills and was settling in. After meeting the housekeeper for keys, instructions, and welcome basket, I went to the shop where I planned to buy a jumper, jacket, sweatshirt, anything to keep the chill off.

"Good morning, I'm Dr. Evelyn Bristol, staying two nights at the Prior's Lodge cottage." I smiled and shivered. "I left my jacket in York." The revelation shouted 'absent-minded professor'. "Do you have any jackets or jumpers for sale?"

The clerk said, "I'm afraid we don't have any clothing items in the shop."

I thanked her and wandered around the shop a bit before finding a plaid wool blanket that would have to do.

As I paid for the blanket and a torch that resembled a lantern, she whipped out an English Heritage vest. "I can offer you this vest, if you promise to be discreet in the wearing of it during your stay." Her facial expression said, "Please don't think you've been hired as a weekend docent."

I'd have gladly taken the job for that vest, in order to ward off the chill of the old stone building and the prospect of even colder air outside.

The cottage promised warmth with plenty of blankets in each bedroom. One room with a double bed and the other sporting twin beds. Kitchen, Sitting/Dining Room. I set the welcome basket on the small table near the kitchen area and took inventory—tea, biscuits, an undoubtedly delicious pepper-encrusted sausage, a couple of apples, an orange, and a bottle of white wine. "Oh. White. Well, I'm sure I can change this for red before she leaves today," my voice sounding my disappointment.

At that moment, I remembered that I had picked up a bottle of New Zealand pinot noir that afternoon. It was still in my satchel nestled in among notebooks, pencils, novel, clothes, and other items. Plenty of room in that satchel with no jacket!

I checked out the kitchen. On the counter, the ubiquitous electric tea kettle, toaster oven, carving set, and dish drainer. In the cabinets beneath, plates, wine glasses, juice glasses, tea cups, silverware, skillet, saucepan, cooking utensils. Milk in the fridge along with two bottles of water. My hopes of drinkable tap water faded.

Not that I'd found any in England so far. The tap water in London or Oxford would put a scum on your tea thicker than your afternoon biscuit. I had to admit, a house without bottled water was also unthinkable in California. Vested by English Heritage and divested of my traveling gear, I left the cottage to explore the ruins.

At the western edge of the North York Moors, the setting for this medieval monastery beggared description; an ideal location for contemplation and all the spiritual as well as intellectual pursuits of these monks. The mist could chill the bones, but even in ruins, the peace and beauty was astounding. The morning marine layer lingered keeping most other people away. Also, it wasn't yet real tourist season in Britain.

Late winter through early spring was the perfect time to travel around as well as work in the archives. Except for commuters, I had been able to move about freely even in London over the last few months. No crowds in the reading rooms or on the trains. I knew that would be changing in about two or three weeks. Another reason, I realized, that I chose this moment to go on my little adventure.

I wandered through the ruins touching the stones of the broken walls, the monastic church, the well house that still tapped the wells on the hillside sending water careening down along well-built stone channels providing fresh water for every monk's cell as well as their latrines. For some reason, I was fascinated with the primary well house, losing track of time sitting on the worn stones that once formed a wall around it.

The water glistening and stirring in the well house remained fresh and clean-looking beneath the leaves scattered on its surface. The worn stones jutted out from the front of the well house and stair-stepped roughly toward the ruins of the monks' cells. An elongated stone with a channel carved down its middle resembled a miniature version of the central gutter of eighteenth-century London streets. But instead of the nasty refuse described by Jonathan Swift, pure clear water flowed from the well house along the channel, from 'step' to 'step' on into the thicker, wider channels of stone carrying water throughout the monastery grounds. A marvel of simple engineering still functioning beautifully after 600 years.

Finally giving up my seat near the well house, I wandered toward the ruins of the small monastic church and monks' cells. Magnificent, even in decline. One spot, a reminder of the human nature of the men who had resided here, appeared around one ruined wall beyond the church.

A window in a wall facing the Great Cloister was barred. The priory gaol. A space for recalcitrant monks to contemplate their futures, recommitting themselves to their vows or being sent elsewhere for further 'instruction'.

I turned and walked back toward the church's stone tower rising above the ruined monastery. Still the focal point of the monastery. I sat on foundation stones near a part of partially destroyed wall where an arched doorway and several window holes remained.

Standing up off the wall, I made my way to what had been the monastery kitchen. All that remained was the fireplace and chimney, for me, reminiscent of the hundreds of lone, stone fireplaces and chimneys still standing on the wind-blown prairies of the Midwestern U.S.

As I walked along, I spotted a small passageway through one wall that a lay brother would use to convey food to a monk in his cell, maintaining the silence and bookmaking of their order. Lost in my reverie of the medieval past, I rounded one half-wall where a natural phenomenon greeted me.

A gorgeous peacock in full plume stood further down the outside wall. An early medieval symbol of immortality, the yearly renewal of its feathers, a resurrection; the 'eyes' on each feather suggesting the all-seeing eyes of God, a slayer of snakes. Interesting, I thought.

How hard it must have been for the monks when Henry VIII and his equally greedy accomplices drove the monks in despair out of their house, their white hoods drawn up against the cold winds of late December 1539.

I shivered now in the misty cold, wondering how the monks had managed the depth of cold of a Yorkshire winter in their stone cells—woolen habits notwithstanding. I pulled the wool blanket out of my satchel and decided to use it to cover a modern bench nearby. I sat down and drew two more items from the satchel, a thermos of steaming hot tea and an egg salad sandwich from Roger and Olivia's shop at the train station in Northallerton.

Yet, I paid only slight attention to my small repast while I mused over the fate of the men forced to leave forever this mystical place. The best of their brethren, especially from the London house, suffering imprisonment and violent execution for refusing to let Henry VIII have his way with religion. Before the monks were driven out, the northern risings took place and threw suspicion on all religious in the north of England. The rebel mob embroiling secular and religious alike, to fight against the shuttering of religious houses, among other Henrician assaults to their lives. Extracting my notebook from my bag, I thumbed through it for connections, if any, to my little quest.

As I read, the daylight across my notebook slowly shifted until I became conscious that it would soon be too dark for me to try to wander up that steep path to the Shrine of Our Lady of Mount Grace (locally known as the Lady Chapel). The directions on a website for the Lady Chapel did not specify which hill to climb behind the monastery but warned that the path up the hill was rough. I hoped to make my way to that chapel without getting lost or injured in the bargain. I tucked my notebook, pencil, thermos, and sandwich leavings back into my satchel before heading to the cottage to settle for the night.

The chill of the twin room intensified and I pulled the blankets up tightly around my chin. At least I didn't have to worry about any spray-painting louts making noise outside. No one seemed to know this place existed except me, the housekeeper for English Heritage, and the woman who worked in the shop. And now, of course, Joe the Cabbie. As I was drifting off, I heard something or someone moving around outside. Fear didn't penetrate, but anger was roiling up.

On a cold night, my sleepwear consisted of wool socks, thick, cotton sweatpants, and a long-sleeved t-shirt, so I was pretty much dressed for anything. I eased out of the bed and slipped on my boots. Grabbing the torch from my satchel, I moved slowly and quietly toward the window closest to where I had heard the sound. I cracked the curtain just an inch, looked and listened. Nothing.

The window was next to the front door of the cottage, so I decided to do one of two things—either rush out with torch light sweeping in front of me or quietly open the door a bit at a time and stay in the dark. I rushed out swinging the light rather more wildly than I'd anticipated. Reminding myself to tap down the adrenalin a peg, I slipped out the door.

Moving forward and sweeping the torch from side to side, more slowly now, I saw a glint off something in the grass to my right. The details of the murder mysteries I read for pleasure and the medieval murders I was researching suddenly brought disturbing images to mind. Shaking these off and commanding my feet to move, I walked toward the now winking light.

One step.

Three steps.

I was practically on top of it before I comprehended what I was seeing. The bottle of white wine supplied by my host was reflecting the light of the torch. "I thought I put that bottle on the porch stoop to take back to the shop. Which I forgot to do when I came back to the cottage." Hearing my own voice in the darkness of the ruined monastery prompted a decision. I grabbed the wine bottle and headed back inside at a fairly good clip.

Back in my room, heavy, full bottle in one hand and unlit torch in the other, I set the bottle on the table with some of the other items from that welcome basket and forgot about the noise outside.

Until it started again.

A sort of shushing sound, like something being dragged along through the grass.

Oh, that's not good, I thought, and shivered.

Then the sound stopped. I stood almost without breathing, holding onto the table. Two minutes went by. Maybe more. A quieter sound, but still a sense that someone was walking through the grass outside my door. I picked up the heavy wine bottle again and moved silently toward the door. I jumped through the door with the torch making great arcs above the ground. Waving the heavy bottle I started shouting, "Who's there? What—"

A fox's eyes glowed in the light of my torch, but he never let go of whatever body he was dragging through the damp grass. Blood, around the fox's mouth now clamped firmly on the hindquarters of something almost as large as the small fox himself. A rabbit. An extremely large one. I walked backward up the stoop until I could put my hand on the door handle. Trying to minimize my size and noise, I pushed the handle down slowly and backed into the cottage. My adrenalin had gone through the roof, so I tried a few breaths before moving away from the door. In. Out. In. Out. When I could breathe normally again, I moved toward the table, aware that I was still being hyper quiet and slow. I set the wine bottle down with more of a thump than I had intended.

Well, that does sleep for awhile, I realized and went about putting the kettle on for a large cuppa with sugar.

The sun sliced through the tiny slats in the blinds on the window, promising a bright day. Though I personally felt less than bright as I peeled myself off the large sofa in the main area where I had finally fallen asleep with only a plush throw for a blanket. I needed to get moving so I could make my way up the hill to the Lady Chapel while the day was clear and dry. It was still early enough that the marine layer could slip over the Cleveland Hills before noon, blotting out the sun and warmth.

I pulled the borrowed vest on over my long sleeve top (the warmest I had with me) and stuffed the plaid blanket back into my day pack along with notebook, torch, water, and the smallest first aid kit ever made. I had to keep the pack light, considering the trudge I'd be making up the slope behind the primary well house to the Chapel.

I propelled myself across the grounds with the stones of the ruined monastery sparkling from the damp early summer morning. As I reached the well house, I stopped and pulled my notebook from my satchel with information about the Lady Chapel.

The access information had guided my preparations for the climb. My mobile was fully charged, the miniature first aid kit nestled in my pack. I was ready for the rough, uneven surface wearing new hiking boots, bought just for the purpose. Confident that I was prepared, I walked on toward the hillside.

At the base of the hill, I detected what looked to be an old trackway about 50 yards from the back of the primary well house. How old was impossible to determine. It could have been the result of pilgrims from the last twenty, or two hundred, years. I merely hoped it would lead me to the Lady Chapel.

The chapel had been restored in the 1950s using, in part, remnants of stone from the destruction of Rosedale Priory, a nunnery surrendered to Henry VIII's greed two months after its "supervision" in 1535. I was eager to get there, so I started up the path.

Steep and uneven, the trackway was, at least, devoid of traffic. In fact, I didn't understand why the website for the Lady Chapel included a caveat about farm vehicles using the track. I kept watch for them but became increasingly distracted trying to maintain balance on the muddy, unlevel surface of the hillside. My new boots were proving worth the money.

As I gained confidence in securing footholds, I could even think about what I might discover among the inscriptions, initials, and prayers left by pilgrims on the original chapel stones, still in situ. Eagerness got the better of me.

I slipped on one of the step-like rocks near the top of the hill.

Although I caught myself before tumbling too far down the slope, I took a bit of a beating. I was a damp, muddy mess by the end of the slide. The borrowed vest would need a good cleaning before I returned it on Monday morning. Still, I reasoned, I'd come too far to turn around. I talked myself back to my feet and back on the track, being especially careful to avoid the slippery rocks this time.

When I reached the top, I pulled the wool blanket out of my satchel and threw it around my shoulders. The damp from my tumble down the hill soaked through my sleeves and pants, chilling the skin beneath. My bones felt cold, and I looked like something out of a zombie movie. Getting a foothold on top of the hill, I hoped no one else had come for an early morning meditation at the chapel.

I needn't have worried about that. The top of the hill, or the slightly flatter part of the hill that I stood on at that moment, revealed no stone chapel or any other building large or small. Just a miniscule clearing with the forest resuming beyond.

Cold, wet, and not a little agitated, I dragged my notebook back out, As I reread the "what to bring" list— first aid kits, proper attire for a country walk, etc., I realized there was no actual map. I simply had made an assumption that the chapel stood on top of the hill abutting the monastery on its east side. I must have conflated the details about the stone well house and the stone chapel, built by the monks nearly 100 years after the founding of the monastery.

I wandered across the top of the hill from where I stood to the start of the tree line declining down the opposite side. No lovely stone chapel with Madonna and Child statue mounted above candles waiting to be lit for a worthy soul. No stained glass windows engraved with the heraldic arms of Katherine of Aragon. No ancient stone altar with sun light slanting through leaded glass panes. No spiritual plane on which to ride for an hour to see what was left of my childhood belief system. No mystery burial outside the chapel walls. Only rocks, mud, and trees. Nothing else.

To say I was discouraged at that moment would be an understatement. How could I, priding myself on being a seasoned traveler, have conflated two different places, and then missed procuring a map?

Although my knowledge of the route from Northallerton to Mt. Grace had surpassed that of the locals, the website for the chapel was mapless. This blunder was totally on me. Prepared, my ass, I thought. I was furious at myself, knowing that at this point it was the better course of valor to turn tail to my warm, little cottage. If only I could locate where I had popped up on top of this hill.

Half an hour later, I found the same track down as I had taken coming up. I still couldn't see anything but trees, mud, and rocks as I slipped and skidded my way down the hillside.

With unspeakable relief, I finally saw the back of the primary well house on the monastery grounds. By that time, I was cold, hungry, and infuriated at my inflated sense of confidence earlier that morning. I couldn't make my way across the grounds and let myself into the cottage fast enough.

After a hot shower to remove all the mud, followed by a nice, long soak in a hot tub, I was feeling human again. I scrambled some eggs to share a plate with beans, toast, and jam. After a third cup of tea with sugar, I was ready to delve back into my notes and go online again to see if I could find map and directions to the Lady Chapel.

A good night's sleep revived me completely, though well-chastened by yesterday's failure. I started out again armed this time with an actual map along with specific instructions from a website on country walks in this part of the North York Moors. I also had called Joe the Cabbie to aid in my quest.

As the crow flies (or straight across the farmer's fields), it was slightly more than a quarter mile from the ruins of the monastery to the Lady Chapel. Since I wanted to save time (the "country walk" taking three hours *in toto*), I recruited Joe and his cab to drop me as close as possible to the private trackway leading up to the Lady Chapel.

On the way, we traveled through the village of Osmotherley (with one stop for a compass and other necessaries) before Joe dropped me near the trackway for my pilgrim's journey to the Lady Chapel. Joe would also pick me up in Osmotherley in three hours and return me to Mount Grace.

The distance from where I now stood on the road up the hill to the Lady Chapel was also supposed to be a quarter mile. I only hoped I could hike up another unlevel, muddy path without tumbling down the slope.

Following a small group of other pilgrims at a distance, I felt disheartened that even so few people were already heading to the Lady Chapel. I wondered how many others I would find milling about up top and how long they would stay.

The six people climbing up the hillside in front of me had only stayed about an hour, departing quickly when mist rolled onto the hilltop. Chilled, too, but determined, I began to explore and take notes.

I wandered around the grounds for a bit before making my way into the Lady Chapel itself. The restored medieval stone walls and the unpretentious accoutrements for worship reflected the austerity of the contemplative life of the Carthusians at Mount Grace as well as the sixteenth-century hermit, once a friar, who entered the hermitage at the Lady Chapel. The meditative spirit was palpable.

A double-arched window with stone mullions bathed the ancient stone altar in light, two candles in modest clay bowls on the altar waiting for Sunday service. The unadorned wooden crucifix on the wall behind the altar created a spiritual simplicity that exemplified the whole space.

I pressed one hand against a large stone near the door. The larger stones in the walls were from the original chapel, some in the same place they had occupied since the late fifteenth century. Sighing deeply and letting my hand fall from the stone, I took the two steps up to the nave.

Walking behind the lectern to the votive stand, I stopped to admire the statue of the Madonna and Child. This statue stood on a stone projecting from the wall above the votive candles. After lighting a candle, I sat down in one of two chairs behind the altar and closed my eyes.

I spent another hour inside the chapel before returning outside to walk the grounds one more time. Then, I headed back down the trackway to meet Joe on the road below.

Joe asked me at least twice on the short drive back to Mount Grace if I needed him any more today or tomorrow. I promised him that I did indeed require a ride back to Northallerton on Monday at about 2PM. That seemed to make his day.

Showered and dressed in my usual bedtime gear, I read over my notes from my time at the Lady Chapel, adding conjectures as I read. The result was, frustratingly, no new revelations about the mystery I believed I had uncovered in a single document housed in a lesser known archive in the early sixteenth-century hand of the hermit of the Lady Chapel.

So, for the umpteenth time, I perused my transcription of the document and went over the notes I'd taken in the archive. If I had made a transcription error, given the nearly illegible hand of the friar/hermit, the document's scribe, I would surely see it this time. Later that night, I discovered I had not made any errors, and I had a revelation.

I knew I'd have daylight until after 9PM so I left the cottage about 7:30. The ruins and grounds were all mine by then, and with my torch, compass, and small trowel in my satchel, I felt prepared for my potential excavation. I also carried a hand drawn map and instructions I had made the night before.

As I crossed the Great Cloister toward the primary well house, I thought about the last days of the monks. Their fears and anger. Their doubts? After years of research on the period, I was convinced that my agnosticism was fully justified. But this bastion of peace and tranquility aligned with the faith of the monks prompted my own doubts. Before I could unpick such thoughts, the sun crossed my little map illuminating it and me. I continued on to the well house.

That took all of five minutes. Plenty of time left if I followed my own instructions and map devised by merging the writings of the sixteenth-century hermit (whom I now believed to be the author of the singular document) and all the archaeological reports on Mount Grace.

I started moving in a straight line up the hill from the wall of the well house facing the hills. Counting steps as indicated by my instructions, I followed the other points I had X'ed on the map. X, it seems, sometimes does mark the spot.

When I reached 150 steps, I was directly at the edge of a cluster of roots and branches of extremely tall trees, the roots running along the surface, engendering offspring as they projected out from the parent tree. This cluster of trees was my first marker.

From there, I began stepping and counting again as I moved around the outside edge of the heavy canopy of branches. I took 75 more steps and stopped. I let my eyes move up the hill and to the left at about a forty-five degree angle. That was from the modern archaeological reports.

This had taken about twenty minutes more. In the midst of the forest on the hillside, the late evening light was fading. Again, I began to worry that my transcription or the archaeological surveys could be error-ridden, or simply bogus. But why would archaeologists, who want to find the truth of a place, make a bogus report? They wouldn't. Carry on, I told myself.

I switched on my torch and followed the beam along what I hoped was a forty-five degree angle. About 50 steps later (I was counting automatically now), the ground felt squishy, moister than only a few steps before. The first spring.

No specifics appeared in the reports by the latest surveyors in the

1990s. But I was certain this was one of the three springs. How to mark it? I needn't have worried.

Moments later, my right toe came into solid contact with a rather large stone protruding slightly from the ground. I bent down to rub my toe as best I could through my thick boot when I noticed marks on the stone. Not chiseled in as some medieval markers had been, but written on with black paint of some sort. MG Spg 1. I was right. This was one of the three springs. Now I had to locate two more. Before I moved, I took a fluorescent orange marking flag from my satchel. That little shop in Osmotherley had been well-provisioned.

Since the document had given me the step count but not numbered the springs, I needed to get my bearings to find the next one. The golden hour after sunset was upon me, so I was soon going to be walking in total darkness except for what light my torch provided.

The light shone over the stone that had stubbed my toe as I pulled my mobile from my jeans pocket and adjusted the camera to flash. Taking first one picture of stone and flag and then another, for good measure, I walked as straight as I could to the right. But how far?

My instructions said that the location of each spring would form a triangle 100 paces per side. That makes an equilateral, right? Breathe, remember your college geometry, I told myself. I continued straight to the right of the first spring, counting out my steps. Again, squishy ground signaled another spring right at the 100-pace mark. It took ten minutes this time to locate a stone stained with the same black paint – MG Spg 2. I left another flag and looked around.

Darkness was complete. I hoped the batteries in my recently purchased torch were not like new car batteries in the States with their short running life. Scanning from the first marker to this one wasn't working. I would have to move away and to the right of my second marker to get the right vantage point for determining the sixty-degree angle I would need for the second side of the equilateral triangle.

Stepping gingerly out of the bog-like ground around the second spring, I took another 35 paces, moving right and up the hill. Throwing light back toward the two spring markers, I tried to calculate the angle. No proper surveying tools would have fit in my bag, even if I remembered how to use them. That landscape arch class had been too long ago. But I had been a damn fine pool player in college, able to "see" the angle of the shots on the table. I fell back on that knowledge and returned to the second spring marker. Squatting on the ground and visualizing a 'pocket' up the hill, I stretched out the arm with the torch, using it as a cue, and calculated the angle. Then I starting counting the paces to the third spring.

When I reached 95, the ground was saturated again. I stopped and flashed my torch over the muck beneath my feet and beyond. I spotted the stone marker within just a few minutes this time and sloshed the half meter to where it protruded above ground level. Stone marker – MG Spg 3. The third flag in place next to the stone, I finished walking back to the first marker of the triangle with relative ease. Now the hard part came. Determining the center of the triangle. I pulled out the instructions and map one more time.

I took 50 paces from the first spring toward the second and stopped. Sticking another orange marking flag into the ground at my feet, I walked to the second spring marker. Another 50 paces with my light pointing toward the third marker. Another marking flag. I practically ran to the third marker, then counted 50 more paces down the last side of the triangle. I had my three vertices. I calculated my shot squatting and pointing as before, then headed for what I determined was the center of the triangle.

Although it was obviously too dark to dig, I was burning to do just that. Still, I consoled myself by taking a few photos of an area about a meter square in the center (as I believed it to be), the flash disturbing the blackness around me. I realized I would have to come out at first light to beat the English Heritage folks and have two hours to work.

In the morning, the marine layer settled in heavily, reminding me of June on a beach in Southern California. But unlike California mist-fog, this wouldn't evaporate before mid-afternoon at the earliest. I needed to get on with my plan, hoping I had taken all precautions necessary to avoid potential problems.

Dressing and gearing up quickly, I went straight to the primary well house and started up the hill. I could barely see until I nearly tripped over that first bloody stone again, my little marking flag drooping from the damp mist. Righting myself, I scanned the ground. My triangle was visible and the center flag, if not flying, at least drooping in style.

I walked toward it and got on my knees. My trowel and brush were in my bag but I figured the trowel would be the only useful tool with all the damp leaves covering the soil. I pulled it from my bag and began to scrape the leaves in an ever widening circle around the marking flag.

As I scraped away, the chill in my hands was nothing to the heat of excitement raising my internal temperature. When I had cleared the leaves from about a one meter square, I started peeling back the soil of my mini trench. I knew I should have contacted English Heritage first thing with what I suspected lay beneath this ground. But that speculation was based primarily on one document. The potential for intellectual embarrassment was too high. My mother's favorite pseudo-biblical line came to mind: "And this too shall pass." I wasn't sure at that moment whether "this" referred to my fear, my protocol error, or, like King Solomon, all I had worked to achieve.

Another half hour went by, as I worked on deepening my trench with all the care I knew it required. Twenty minutes or a lifetime later, a glimmer broke the blackness of the soil. I sat back on my heels and peered down into the trench. Definitely, a glint of metal. I reached in my bag for the brush I'd bought in Osmotherley.

Ever so carefully, I swept the tip of the brush across the widening metal surface. In another hour, not only a silver gilt chalice had emerged from the bottom of my trench but a copper and gilt pyx. I took the first full breath of that morning.

The last hermit, living in the hermitage at the Lady Chapel and the scribe of the document I had found, was former Franciscan friar Thomas Parkinson. He occupied the chapel's hermitage from 1515 until the dissolution of the monastery.

Parkinson had entered the hermitage after it was rebuilt by Katherine of Aragon, when still Henry VIII's queen. After Katherine's physical and quasi-legal annulment from Henry VIII in 1533, only six years would remain before the monks and the hermit would be forced to surrender their enclosures. At some point in those final years, Parkinson decided to save these two amazing pieces from the grasp of Henry VIII's minions and all who claimed ownership of the grounds thereafter. The poor hermit must have written the note that eventually made its way to that little known archive soon after he buried these, for him, sacred artifacts and before his departure from here in December 1539.

And no wonder he chose this spot. Three springs would have made the ground between them much easier to dig at any time of year and a safe remove from the ruin of the religious lives of the monks and the hermit soon to come.

Finding these artifacts meant that it *was* imperative for me to contact the proper authorities. After I reburied chalice and pyx, of course.

A year later, sitting on my little patio sipping a lovely California pinot noir, I flipped through the journal containing my article, "Finding the Friar's Stash: A fortuitous *aventure* in Yorkshire."

According to my article, I had determined that the scribe of the document was, indeed, Thomas Parkinson, former friar and then hermit of the Lady Chapel. Although the scribal hand was difficult, the text having been written hastily —under imminent danger?—I was able to transcribe it. This document revealed the location of the burial place of two significant artifacts.

From my transcript and notes, English Heritage archaeologists had been able to "discover" a silver chalice and a copper and gilt pyx with a small finger bone inside. Historians argued that the bone must have belonged to Richard Methley, a Carthusian of Mount Grace, who has been called the last great mystic before the Reformation.

The chalice and pyx, and especially Methley's finger bone, would have been deemed sacred by the hermit who buried them and left us this note. Both artifacts were dated c. 1527, ironically, the year of Richard Methley's demise and the beginning of the end of a thousand years of Catholicism in England.

Homecoming

Crisis Management

Jude's sister, Susan, had wanted nothing more to do with the place after her husband apparently got out of bed one night, took a shotgun off the rack, walked outside into the old well-house, and blew his brains out.

The police had made their obligatory call so that the coroner could report, death by self-inflicted gunshot wound. They had offered Susan the phone number for a crime-scene clean-up crew which she wouldn't call. Susan wouldn't even come near the old stone building set between the farmhouse and the barnyard. So Jude stayed on long enough after the funeral to put on a store-bought haz-mat suit and clean the inside of the well-house by herself. It was a nasty mess.

Bill, the dead brother-in-law, had obviously sat down right inside the door with his back to the cramped space inside the building. Skin and hair and brain tissue exploded all over the top of the machine that pumped water up from the bottom of the well and through the pipes. As she cleaned, Jude wondered if somehow a piece of him had oozed into a loose o-ring of the pipe that carried the water indoors. She cleaned more enthusiastically after that getting her brother-in-law's bits out along with decades of dirt, animal hair, and God-knew-what from all over the inside of the place.

Jude's not bringing her fifteen-year-old daughter, Abby, to Bill's funeral was justified. Abby couldn't remember Bill anyway, and Jude knew it would be a frenzy of grief, guilt, and shame from Susan and her kids. Curling her lips at the bloody mess all around her, Jude was, indeed, glad her daughter was still in California.

Only a few weeks elapsed after Jude returned to her own home in the Bay Area before she received a call from her sister pleading, begging Jude to buy Susan's share of the family place. All Susan wanted to do was get away from that house and their hometown, where she had lived her entire life. Jude certainly understood that feeling but never thought anything could get Susan out. When Susan called, she had already started the process for her own retirement from the junior high where she had been working as a secretary even before she and Bill were married

Well, I suppose without Bill, and the kids grown and gone, Jude considered, Susan has no one to boss around. I should have guessed she'd head for Oregon to annoy her adult children.

By the end of July, Jude had bought Susan out of her share of the house. Only because her sabbatical was starting that Fall could Jude even imagine it at all. Now here she was, standing just inside the gate of the old farmhouse wondering why. Jude turned toward the road, staring through time remembering the farm's red horse barn and windmill in the pasture just beyond the house where now modern houses stood.

"What the hell am I doing?" she cried aloud, trying to force herself to turn toward the house and walk in. At least Abby isn't here yet, she sighed. I need to get used to this place first so that when she comes in a couple of weeks for the school year, I can convince her she'll like it.

Right. Sure, I can. *I* never liked the house, why should Abby? It's classic well-appointed farmhouse—oak floors, stone fireplace, slate hearth, bedrooms upstairs, one bath up and one down, big farm kitchen, dining room, entryway, and a three-room dirt-floored basement. Oh, that basement. The prime place of my childhood fears and nightmares.

Jude shook her head from side to side and began to speak sternly to her inner child. Ridiculous. There's nothing in the basement except dirt, mice feces, and old rotten—okay, nevermind, turn and step.

That thought made her laugh as she remembered watching a Three Stooges skit with her dad with that "slowly I turned" tag line, ending of course in slapstick hilarity, an act, where no one really got hurt. Certainly, no one died. But more than one person reportedly died here.

Her Uncle Jack's ghost stories haunted the house of her childhood, especially the story about the Hanged Man. Now Bill had blown his brains out in the well-house, a structure Jude considered benign, good even, bringing water from the under ground well right into their glasses. Jude shuddered as she thought about a real ghost inhabiting the little, stone building.

She turned abruptly, walked swiftly to the front door, and slid the house key into the lock. She made a mental note to have another key made for Abby. Maybe a new one for herself, too. This was Bill's key which her sister had been more than willing to give away. It *was* kind of creepy at that, she thought, as she stepped inside the entryway and set her bags down. Before she could take another step, the quiet, the absence of the smell of her mother's cooking and baking that used to greet her whenever she walked in that door, made her panic. She took a strained, deep breath and went toward the kitchen on the right.

Before Bill's suicide, Jude hadn't been in the house since her mother died nearly ten years before. There was always a reason, an excuse for her absence after that—attending a conference, writing a book, giving a reading, semester starting, finishing—always something to prevent her from taking her sister up on an invitation to spend Christmas. Now, the house was hers alone with the ghost of every Christmas past and then some. The Hanged Man. Bill. Her parents, her grandparents. What the hell was I thinking? she chastised herself.

Jude had gone through her list after Susan's first begging phone call: 1) get the next book finished during her sabbatical leave, 2) go on with her own plans, and 3) tell her sister to sell the house and send Jude her share. Their hometown was a university town with lots of possible buyers who wouldn't know its recent, sordid history—maybe.

But, when Jude called her sister back with these reasonable arguments firmly in mind, she had said instead, "O.K., I'll buy you out."

The next morning she texted her best friend, Linda, to try to get Linda to come over and talk her out of this terrible commitment. To tell Jude to call Susan back and say, just kidding. When Linda arrived, Jude only said, "I'm buying my sister out of the family place so she can move on from her husband's death." Linda hugged Jude for being the best sister ever and that was that.

But, Jude didn't feel like the best anything ever. She felt confused and angry. As so often in the past on her own, her impulse now was to sit down and write. Jude was convinced that writing was the best approach to any problem—either write or clean something. None of her working class, middle-American family ever really understood the writer and scholar in her, her life of the mind. As a high school history teacher, Bill should have been sympathetic, but, if he was, he was a silent ally, merely shrugging, smiling, and leaving the room when the others started in.

Jude's life did not produce much as far as they could tell. She read, wrote, and taught and made no serious money. When her daughter, Abby, was born fifteen years ago, they thought there might be hope for Jude. Although they were forced to admit that she was a good mother, they didn't think her work should still take up so much of her time.

But, since she and Abby *seemed* to be happy, they never harassed her about it. Well, not after a few years. They also would never listen to her talk about her life beyond what she did with Abby.

After Abby was born and before Jude's mother died, Jude and Abby used to visit every summer. Jude's then husband, Alex, was always too busy with his work to come along. Jude's mother and the rest of the family were fine with that. They didn't like Alex any more than he liked them. But he might have served Jude as a nice buffer during those visits when she became a one-woman audience for her family to chant their trials and tribulations.

They ranted about secrets uncovered on this or that person whom she was supposed to know or remember. Her daughter's presence would distract the family during the day, but after Abby went to bed, Jude became a human sounding board. No one ever, even once, asked about her life outside of motherhood—her teaching, what she was researching, writing, if she and Alex were getting along, who their friends were. Instead, it was: "You remember, so and so, oh, sure you do. She/He…" Then they were off on who died, who had kids or grandkids, whose kids or grandkids were successful (that meant making money), in jail, or in default of family feeling.

Jude was often tempted during those moments to go into lecture-mode and recount all that she had accomplished or experienced since her last visit, in an uninterrupted monologue until their eyes glazed over, or they made some excuse to leave the room. But, she never could bring herself to be that assertive, rude, whatever you want to call it, with her family. Something about being the youngest child, the transient relative, made her smile or frown (whichever seemed appropriate), and nod at all they said and did.

They never even asked how she had managed financially or physically when she moved from grad school to her first two jobs, from coast to coast to coast, or how she and Abby coped after Jude and Alex divorced five years ago. They didn't seem to wonder about her at all. So now, in that silent house, the absence of those voices reverberated.

Susan had cleared out completely and even cleaned. Relieved of that chore at least, Jude began to wander from room to room, downstairs then upstairs. But when she reached the room that Susan had called Bill's "man-cave" (a term Jude detested in every fiber of her being), she was shocked to find it looking pretty much as it had the last time she was there—full of the detritus of a traditional man's life.

Her sister would always proclaim, "That's Bill's hidey hole from the family, and I'm not touching anything in it!" Apparently, that statement continued to be enforced post-mortem, their two grown children not defying their mother in that or anything concerning their father after his suicide. They were guilt-stricken and ashamed about a father who had committed suicide. Like their mother, they just wanted to forget.

Jude sighed audibly and felt the hairs on the back of her neck stand up as her sigh broke the silence of the house. To dispel her discomfort, she physically turned on her heel and practically marched down the stairs. Since Susan had taken all the furniture, no table or chair presented itself as a place to write so Jude called on her "clean it" approach in Bill's room.

Her sister did leave behind a stack of unused boxes from her move to Oregon. Probably because she refused to take any of Bill's things from that bloody room, Jude thought, as she picked up a few boxes to carry up the stairs. I suppose I'll just put all his stuff in these boxes and cart the lot off tomorrow. Her cell phone rang disrupting the thought as it flitted through her head.

"Hello? Oh, Linda. So good to hear your voice! Any chance you have a burning desire to come to the Midwest?" She let her friend know what was going on at her end and secured Linda's assurance that she would be coming to see Jude at some point during the winter break.

"Where's Rufus?" she wondered aloud as she clicked off her phone.

She looked around the old dining room where Susan had left the boxes, but no Rufus. Their cat had come with Jude since Abby was staying with her father over the summer.

Rufus had spent a good part of the morning running up and down stairs (amenities their house in California did not have), peering into each room, sniffing around the fireplace, and checking every closet and corner of the house. But he didn't normally stray far from Jude.

"Rufus?" She called and whistled, the only cat she ever knew to respond to a whistle like a dog. Rufus was an unusual cat in general.

When she rescued him from the streets near their home in California, he was about a year old. A wound on his shoulder made him limp a bit, and his long, black hair was matted and dirty. He looked rough, but, he responded well to the vet's treatment and to Jude and Abby's loving care. Although he didn't resist their picking him up, doctoring his wound, or taking him to and from the vet in a carrier, he was cautious at first and stingy with his affection. In a few months, he realized that staying indoors with these humans meant he would never be hungry, thirsty, or lonely again.

In the two years since his rescue, Rufus had filled out nicely. His short, stout legs and wide head still made him look like a fighter, but Jude had discovered that was a bluff. Rufus looked tough and strutted tough but was a big baby, who needed his special bed in Abby's room and constant attention when either mother or daughter was at home. Jude was forced to close her study door to keep him out when she was deep into her work or he would scatter papers and books everywhere as he rolled around among them to get her attention. His fur, now well-kempt and shining from his privileged life, turned out to be black only on the top half of his body. His belly from chin to butt was a beautiful dark silver. He was a looker and knew it.

"Rufus," she called more loudly the second time, and the cat came flying up from the basement, his once shining fur covered with cobwebs and dust.

"Oh, no. I meant to keep you out of that basement. God knows what's down there."

The old basement provided the stuff of Jude's nightmares during childhood, and she always tried to find some reason for not going down by herself. Her mother, the most practical of women, would have none of Jude's fears and often sent Jude, "who was just being silly" to fetch jars of home-canned fruits and vegetables stored in the basement cabinets.

Jude hated the sparsely-illuminated spaces in the three basement rooms; she hated the smell of the dirt floor; and she detested the taste of dust left in her mouth after a trip to the basement. But Jude loved the smell of the earth out of doors, in the garden, in the fields—just not what happened when it was covered by a house.

Her childhood memories included the sounds of traps snapping and rats screaming, the rats driven into the basement from the barns and fields during spring or summer rains. Jude also clearly remembered snakes—rattlesnakes from the wood piles, black snakes from everywhere, garden snakes of several varieties—too many had found their way into that basement and even into the house.

When Jude was seventeen, she was getting ready to go out on a date. Dating always made her nervous, and she would have to go to the toilet seemingly every five minutes before she finally dressed and went out. This night was no exception, but, when she sat down to pee (one more time) in the upstairs bathroom, she suddenly felt the need to look down at her feet. A baby rattlesnake curled up and ready to strike stared back. She didn't think about her parents' warnings—don't move or cry out, stay still, it will leave. Without thinking at all, she jumped up and ran, tugging at her underwear, half up and half down her legs. After he disposed of the snake, her dad had said that the little rattler must have slithered in from the woodpile where the top logs and the slight cracks in the foundation met.

Of course, the adult Jude was rational. After all, she reasoned, she had for years been a member of many animal welfare organizations and no longer believed that the only good snake was a dead snake. Her animal activism had encouraged her to find alternative ways of living with the natural world. No fumigation for mice, rats, or insects. No murdering snakes, just because they lived nearby. Still, she really didn't want Rufus or herself encountering one in that wretched basement.

"What *am* I going to do about the basement?" Rufus stared at her when she spoke, as confused about it all as she was. "If I want to sell this place someday (why wouldn't I?), that basement will have to be completely redone."

Susan complained for years about the basement flooding with every big storm. They had to install a permanent skimmer pump down there after the flooding started. That was shortly after the developers began building new houses on the land their grandmother sold when Jude was about twelve, only the acre around the house remaining in the family. The developers caused more problems by diverting the flow of the river scheming to increase the attraction of the property for potential buyers. Those homeowners became less enamored of their riverside property when the river flooded every spring. Jude always believed her mother secretly felt this justified her resentment of the sale of her beloved farm.

An hour later, Jude was just scratching the surface of the debris (as she thought of it) in Bill's den (she preferred the old-fashioned term used by her parents) when hunger and thirst interrupted. She hoped that Chinese place in the strip mall nearby was still there with its drive-thru window. Jude was in no mood to spend time cleaning herself up to go out to eat. Susan had left the stove and refrigerator at least, but stocking up would have to wait until tomorrow.

"I'll get a bottle of pinot noir and some good cheese, on my dinner run, Rufus, but that's for later. Now, we need real food and bottles of water."

Oh. Water. The word brought Jude's mind back to the basement.

The flooding in the basement was not the only water problem in the old farmhouse. Their water supply came from what her mother had always called "underground rivers." Jude had thought at her last visit that, whatever the source, it was petering out or polluted. The water from the tap tasted to her like metal shavings and dirt. Now it had brother-in-law mixed up in it. Another sigh got her up and down the stairs. Rufus reluctantly gave up his game of slide-on-the-loose-papers to follow Jude downstairs.

"You have to stay here, Ruf. I'll be back in a flash," she promised with a quick scratch on the cat's head.

If a cat could say, "pfft," Rufus did as he turned with his tail in the air to run back up the stairs.

When Jude finished her food, she rinsed the boxes, pulled the metal handle out of each one, and nested the boxes together. Then she looked for the household recycle bins. "Oh, that's a habit I hope we don't have to break."

She remembered then that her sister did not recycle. "Too much trouble" seemed enough reason for Susan. No big bins, then, Jude realized as she added bins to her list for tomorrow's shopping. Tonight, I'll use Bill's miniature recycle bin.

Bill had never fought with his wife over any major issues although Jude often suspected that he had more environmental sense than his wife. Proven today, she thought, when I found those stacks of newspapers tied with string tucked away in the cabinets on one wall in the den along with a very small bin full of aluminum cans. He must have run his recyclables out to the one recycling center in town whenever

Susan was out of the house. Why not just convert her? Jude wondered. Though she knew the answer before the question finished resonating in her head.

She had tried for years to convince Susan to be more environmentally conscious, to be more socially conscious. But Susan was in a world of her own, a fictional world created by Susan to maintain Susan's illusions of her own perfection and God-given happiness. Any issue that required her to think beyond her own well-controlled perspectives of life just had to be left unconsidered. Whatever Bill might have believed (and clearly he had his own mind about recycling), he kept it from Susan. Susan's optimistic outlook was really self-delusion. Jude often thought one of them must have been adopted. She and Susan didn't think alike at all, didn't even look alike.

Jude was sixteen years younger than her sister, born a year after an older brother Jude had never known was killed in Vietnam. Jude suspected that her parents had tried to have another son but wound up, instead, with this constantly questioning, assertive girl. As a child, Jude would argue with anyone and ask so many questions that her parents were constantly scolding her to stop talking everyone's ear off. They never understood her desire to know. Jude learned to compartmentalize thoughts and ideas to return to them later when she had time for deeper consideration. Good training for a scholar-teacher. As she set the nested boxes and metal handles on the counter to be dealt with later, Jude placed thoughts of the past behind her. For now.

Rufus's head appeared out of the partially open door of the pantry, empty now except for the cat. "Come on, you. Let's go back upstairs." As if he understood every word, the cat strolled out of the pantry and proceeded to follow Jude out of the kitchen and up the stairs.

A swish and a thump woke Jude out of a strange dream about being buried alive. Night filled the room so she couldn't, at first, see if the sound was in the room or elsewhere in the house or just in the dream. She had fallen asleep on a pile of old papers intended for a box. As she pulled a shred of yellowed paper from her face, she reached for her phone to shine a small circle of light around her so she could make it to the light switch without stepping on anything important, like Rufus.

The screen on her phone lit up the space around her, and Rufus's green eyes shone in the darkness nearby. Jude shuffled along the edge of the boxes to flip the switch. The light so bright for a second that she couldn't see. Then, everything sorted, and she saw Rufus standing indignantly on a loose pile of papers with his right foot plucking at something in the mess.

"What do you have there?" she said to the cat as visions of mice, spiders and snakes came into her head.

She shook them off and walked over to Rufus still tugging away at what turned out to be a broad piece of elastic around an old three-ring binder. Relieved and not a little irritated, Jude retrieved the binder from the cat's tenacious grasp and sat down with it on the floor next to Rufus.

When Jude opened the binder, she found newspaper clippings and slight, scribbled notes in the margins next to the clippings on a dozen pages or so. She recognized Bill's handwriting in the marginal notes but thought, at first, that he was doing what she did in photo albums and scrapbooks, making notes so as not to forget who or what was in the picture or piece of memorabilia.

She squinted at a note next to a clipping on the third page with the headline: "Murder trial reconvenes tomorrow with final arguments." Maybe it was some historical research Bill was doing for himself or his classes, she thought. The newspaper clippings' dates were all in the summer of 1968 when Bill was, what? 18? We didn't know him until he started dating Susan several years later.

Another note caught her attention about two-thirds of the way down the far left column. Jude kept turning the pages in the binder and reading various notes running alongside most of the articles. All the clippings were about the same trial.

The first article carried the picture of a teenage boy and claimed that a drifter was standing trial for his murder. Apparently, the murder had happened along the north shore of the river. The second article's photo angled across the crowded courtroom. Jude searched the faces until she spotted two or three teenagers standing near the back. One of the boys appeared to Jude a possible younger version of Bill. The grainy photo made it hard to tell. The boy she thought might be Bill had that late 60s' bang suggesting longer hair without getting kicked out of school for it.

No surprise, she thought, if Bill or any other boys were in that courtroom, most adolescent boys being half "ghoul."

As she said the last word aloud, she felt a chill literally slide up her back. Rufus looked up from the paper he was boisterously shredding with his teeth.

"Sorry, Ruf." When she spoke, she had uncurled herself right onto the paper Rufus was tearing up. He glared at her rudeness.

Jude stood up then and carried the binder down the stairs with her, Rufus now close on her heels. She needed some water and planned to sit at the kitchen table where the light was better. But, the round oak table, the centerpiece of their country kitchen, was gone along with every other stick of furniture other than what was in Bill's den. Susan had felt it her right to take all of their parents' furniture along with her own.

First thing in the morning, I'm going to that used furniture store I passed tonight, she thought. I'll get enough furniture to get us through this year. That means tonight, I'll have to sleep in Bill's overstuffed den chair. Rufus appeared skeptical but couldn't be left out of whatever game she might be playing.

"Oh, not good, Rufus. Cats can see ghosts, and Bill's might be hanging around his den right now," she tried to laugh but hadn't meant to say the last bit out loud.

It was far too disturbing a thought to verbalize. Even at her most rational moments, the atmosphere of that house, especially at night, could turn her back into the child, frightened by Uncle Jack's stories.

One of her mother's brothers perversely delighted in telling all the nieces and nephews chilling ghost stories about the house and farm buildings around it. According to Uncle Jack, the old well, long abandoned, was haunted by the ghosts of the first Kansas settlers who had dug it and lost two children to its murky depths—"Beware!" he would wail. One late summer night, a farm hand had snuck out to the silo where he'd earlier sunk a ceramic jug pierced along the top to let the sorghum alcohol seep in. As he leaned down into the silo to retrieve it, he fell in, drowning in the quicksand-like silage—"Beware!" Another farm hand, despondent over his money troubles crawled up into the rafters of the old barn, now this house (Uncle Jack always pointing dramatically toward the farmhouse), and hanged himself. Isn't that your bedroom, Jude—"Beware!" Uncle Jack was quite the performer enjoying the squeals of fear made by his young audience. The problem was that Jude was the youngest and had to go up to that same bedroom, first and alone.

"I wonder if I ever got a full night's sleep growing up in this house, Rufus!"

With a heavy sigh this time, she grabbed a bottle of water from the refrigerator and went back upstairs with Bill's binder. She checked her phone for emails and any missed calls but found none. She had texted Abby when she arrived but still no response. She settled into the big chair and opened the binder again.

The dozen or so pages contained probably three or four clippings each, depending on the size of the articles. She read every article and all the notes, with Bill's main comments, "Not the whole story" and "Lies" repeatedly scrawled on the page. "Was the murdered kid one of his friends? But why, when an article talks about the suspected events, do you always seem to object?" Jude wondered aloud and looked around involuntarily, still hoping Bill wouldn't be hanging around to answer her questions.

"Bill, I don't have time for your issues and mine, too," she shouted into the dark room.

Jude closed the binder abruptly and tossed it on the side table next to the chair. Her burn pile. Standing up, she stretched before heading back down the stairs. Rufus had fallen asleep in one of the boxes and lifted one eyelid to watch her go.

"Come on, Rufus. Ruf? Okay, stay where you are, lazy." Jude went down to the kitchen, turning lights on all along the way.

When she came back to the den, she had a bottle of wine, a small brick of Red Leicester cheese, and a cheap wine glass from a store at the mall. She sipped the wine and nibbled the cheese, all the while staring at the closed binder. Finally, she picked it up again.

"This is what I do, right? I study early books, manuscripts, documents of all kinds trying to tease out their secrets. Surely, I can do that with these relatively modern newspaper clippings," she considered this aloud. Rufus didn't respond.

She started on the first page and read each article carefully making mental notes of names and other particulars that might help her in an archival search of court documents, if they were in the public record and available online.

"Wait a minute, earlier I spotted some high school yearbooks in here somewhere. Where are those?"

Jude got up carefully negotiating boxes and loose piles of papers as she made her way to a small bank of cabinets. The second cabinet door she opened proved her memory correct. Bill's last high school yearbook. She started thumbing through the senior pictures and found a young Bill smiling broadly at the camera. Then, she saw her brother's picture. Her parents always kept this same picture hanging on the wall in the living room along with her sister's and, eventually, her own senior picture. Jude stared at and through his image, looking into a past she hadn't known. Then she shook herself and began to turn the pages of the yearbook.

About 30 pages into the yearbook, she found Bill standing with three other boys, heads down as if contemplating the pieces of paper in their hands, or praying. Very strange photo, she thought, then saw the caption. Oh, high school All-Americans.

Jude was fairly certain that Bill had never even mentioned playing football in high school. Some of the guys she had known in her high school years, even though many years after Bill's time, had talked of little else when she ran into them a year or two after graduation. All of those guys had failed to achieve glory beyond high school. Maybe all the years Bill taught at the high school and did his duty supporting its 'champion' football team meant he understood the limitations of glory, Jude considered. She stared at the picture of the three boys; all three were familiar to her.

"Of course. One is my brother, Robbie, standing on the right with Bill in the middle. How could I possibly know the other boy? Unless." Her habit of speaking her thoughts aloud when she was working was disrupting Rufus's sleep.

She laid the yearbook down and picked up the binder again. The first page of clippings included one with a picture of the murdered boy, Freddie Sanborn.

"That's the kid standing on the other side of Bill in the yearbook photo. Mystery solved!" Jude startled Rufus and herself as her comment rang out through the dark, empty house. "So not a history project but a *memento mori* for Bill. Poor guy. Distraught over his friend's murder. But, why keep writing 'lies' or 'not the whole story' next to certain articles?"

Rufus suddenly plopped down on top of the binder as if to remind her that they needed to go to bed, or chair, as it would be tonight.

"Alright, Ruf, let's put these aside. I'll crawl up in this chair after I bring your bed in here. It's late!" Her phone startled both of them as it suddenly binged, lighting up with a text from Abby, clearly unaware of the two-hour difference in time zones.

In the morning, Jude called her friend, Linda, to tell her about the scrapbook and Bill's glosses. Linda thought the mystery had been solved by the pictures in the yearbook, but Jude wasn't convinced.

"I don't know. It's Bill's notes written repeatedly next to certain articles that bother me. Or maybe I'm just trying to avoid my own work with this little mystery."

They talked on about Jude's book and Linda's own research project for another thirty minutes before ending their conversation.

After that, Jude grabbed the keys to Bill's car from the peg board near where the family phone still hung on the wall. The car was part of the buy-out. She could use it this year and sell it before she went home or if, when, she sold the house. She still needed to go to the store to get food and other supplies and search for a few pieces of essential furniture. But before she left the house she went online and ordered two Caspers, one for herself and one for Abby. After her bone-crunching sleep in Bill's chair, Jude determined to buy the mattresses before Abby arrived.

"Ah, well, Rufus, I'll have to tough it out in Bill's chair a little longer. We can put the new mattress on the floor with yours in the old master bedroom next to the den."

As long as she could remember, her parents had occupied these two rooms at the top of the stairs. The reminiscence was tinged with sadness as her thoughts of her parents always were.

As Rufus ran off down the hall, Jude tried to recall when Bill and Susan had moved in with their parents. Ah, right, when Philip was just a few months old, she remembered. They said they were just waiting for the right house at the right price. Funny, a couple of decades later that house still had not materialized. After each of my parents died, Bill, Susan, and their kids filled the vacant spaces, including those two rooms which became Bill's den. A place where he could read and "putter," as Susan frequently told me. Where, no doubt, the poor guy could get away from Susan's manic optimism.

Jude turned her attention to boxing up the last of Bill's stuff so that, tomorrow, she could take the clothes to a Salvation Army, the books to a used bookstore, and the bundled newspapers and little bin to the recycling center. Any, more sensitive papers she could take to the burn bin.

Toward evening, Jude took some papers, including the scrapbook, out the back door toward the burn barrel, still in the place her grandfather had placed it decades ago. She realized that she was actually surprised to find it still there with the house in the city limits now. What she hadn't thought about were matches. One more sigh turned her back toward the house.

The matches had always been kept in the last kitchen drawer next to the basement door where the steps led to the outer door. As she walked, Jude wished, ever so briefly, that she still smoked. When she had, many years ago, she always carried matches in her jeans pocket. Now she only hoped that Susan left some random matches for her use. Amazingly, she found a book of matches stuck in the crack in the very back of that kitchen drawer. Would they still light, she wondered?

Rufus sat on the kitchen counter glaring at her for going outside again without him. He knew it was his right as a cat to resent her comings and goings in spite of his own actual indifference to such disruptions.

Jude held the matches tightly against the pile of papers and the scrapbook as she made her way back to the burn barrel, night pressing in around the horizon making it difficult to see. The darkness of the barrel's depths obscured any remnants of recent burning although she didn't imagine that Susan would have dirtied her hands by using it. After staring into the depths of the empty barrel for a few minutes, Jude dropped the papers and tossed a match, then a second one on top of the pile. The flames were so bright for a moment that they blinded her, yet so far down in the barrel that no one else would see anything more than a quick flash of light. Holding the scrapbook firmly to her chest, she turned and walked back toward the house in the dark.

II

Discoveries

After the initial cleaning of Bill's den, toting away the remains from there, and finding some furniture to get them through the year, Jude threw herself into her book. When she finished revisions three months later, Jude popped her revised manuscript into the publisher's Dropbox folder and leaned back in the cheap office chair purchased with the other pieces her first week in the house. Now, Jude ran her hand through her short curls and sighed.

"Okay, Rufus, there it goes. They promised me the copyedited chapters one at a time starting in about six weeks. Let's celebrate."

Jude stood up and looked around for her cat who usually stayed pretty close to her while she was working. Rufus wasn't in the chair or on his bed or hers in the next room.

"Rufus," she called turning toward the outer door.

No Rufus. Jude walked through the door and down the upstairs hallway toward the south end of the house. Rufus sometimes chased his toys down that way. No Rufus. She walked back down the hallway and started down the stairs when Rufus came flying up them.

"Rufus, seriously, boy, you have to stop disappearing. I'm worried you'll manage to sneak down into that nasty basement and find a cat-sized crack that I haven't discovered yet."

Rufus had stopped on the top step and swished his tail at her, as if to say, "If I want to, I will."

Jude came back up the few stairs she had descended and headed for the bathroom. If she took a shower, she knew she'd feel less stiff from sitting at her computer for hours finishing her revisions. Now she required hot water and her coconut cleanser all over her body.

"That should relax these tense muscles enough to get a decent night's sleep after we celebrate, Ruf."

But, she knew that when Abby came home from school, she would be complaining, asking for the hundredth time why her mother had forced her to leave her friends and come to this place where school started obscenely early—August instead of after Labor Day like her high school in California, where they took a brunch break in the outdoors, blah, blah, blah. Jude sighed at the thought knowing that her daughter's teen angst would put a damper on any kind of celebratory mood she might muster. Before her daughter arrived about two months ago for the school year, Jude had talked to no one "live" but store clerks or the woman at the drive-thru Chinese restaurant.

Jude no longer kept in touch with her few high school friends. Her college friends, the same. Her close friendships from grad school endured, but those friends were scattered and as busy as Jude was. Jude's closest friend now was Linda, a colleague with whom she could share elements of her personal as well as her professional life. And

Linda was coming to visit Jude in December when Abby flew back to spend some of the Christmas vacation with her Dad. Still weeks away.

The sudden noise of her chair rolling across the wood floor scared Rufus who was eyeing a bird sitting on the porch roof on the other side of the window. Trying to convey his disgust at her interruption of his concentration made him fall off the sill; the bird, on the other side of the glass, then flew away. The comedy made Jude laugh so hard she had to search the room for a box of tissues to wipe tears from the corners of her eyes.

The box sat on the back counter under the small bank of cabinets. As she reached for one, she remembered that she had put Bill's scrapbook in one of these cabinets after changing her mind about incinerating it.

The scrapbook with the elastic cord still in place appeared forlorn sitting in the otherwise empty cabinet.

"I'd almost forgotten about this book. Why didn't I burn it? Oh, well, maybe now I can find some diversion in its contents until my galleys arrive. Contents might be too strong a term for the artlessly arranged articles taped onto the dozen or so pages inside. The work of an 18-year-old boy." Rufus, still disgruntled, ignored her.

Jude extracted the book from the cabinet and sat down in the overstuffed chair. After a few minutes, she reached for a legal pad and pencil to take some notes. She forgot about taking a shower and, instead, spent the next couple of hours reading each newspaper article carefully, jotting down headlines and dates along with Bill's comments.

When Abby came home, she was actually happy. Her new friend, Emily, who had a car, was coming to pick Abby up at 7 o'clock so they could go to the library downtown to study.

"At the library, really, Abby?" Jude couldn't disguise her amusement disguised as skepticism.

"Mother, Emily needs my help studying for that Chem test. Chem is easy for me so she asked me to help." Abby's eyes narrowed, challenging.

"Can I meet Emily before you go out. I never heard you talk about her before. Is she nice? Smart? What do her parents do?"

"Mom, seriously, we are not 10! I don't know what her parents do, but, yes, she is very nice. She was new last year. We have Chem together and have our lunch break during that class so we have been talking for a couple of weeks. I just didn't tell you so you wouldn't say 'I told you so'." Now her daughter was laughing at herself and smiling at Jude.

"I do want to meet her before you head off to the library tonight. Be home by 10:00, please."

"O.K. and you know I will be home on time. Rufus can't sleep when I'm not home." As she said this Rufus swished his fluffy, black tail around her legs and then flopped on his side in a curl so she could scratch his belly. "Did you finish your book today?"

"Yes. I thought we might go out to dinner someplace special to celebrate."

"Great."

Jude woke up early the next morning to get her daughter off to school. As she fixed some breakfast for Abby, she kept thinking about her dream—someone chasing her with a baseball bat along the riverbank. I guess I shouldn't read those articles in the scrapbook before I go to bed, she realized.

But the dreams had stirred a memory from her first encounter with the scrapbook. She decided that she would go downtown to the local history museum after she dropped Abby at school. On the way out the door, she grabbed an apple for her breakfast.

Jude parked her car near the courthouse and walked across the street into the museum. She thought they might have more information on the murder case than she had been able to find online. A local search might help her fill in the blanks in Bill's scrapbook. A small bank of computers lined one wall with a sign over them that said Public Access to the Watson Historical Museum Catalogue. She sat down at one of the empty chairs and started to scroll through the subject headings. In half an hour, she was seated in one of the carrels lining the opposite wall with a couple of books and a box of clippings marked "Sanborn Murder Case Files." A few hours later, she returned the books and box to the librarian, put her legal pad away, and headed out the door.

I can try to collate these notes with the ones I've taken on Bill's collection of articles and see if I can figure out why he would hold onto them for all these years, she decided. I don't remember him ever talking about this, but, of course, Susan would not have allowed such a morbid topic in her presence. And when was I ever around Bill that Susan wasn't close by? And why would this murder, sad as it would have been for Bill to lose a friend in this way, have made him cut out newspaper articles, write comments (even such brief ones) in the margins, and keep the binder in his den for four decades without ever talking about it? Surely the summer I visited after my book on medieval murder cases was released, this would have come up. Oh, that's right, no one ever asked me what I was working on or looked at the copies of the books that I sent them. Jude wrinkled her whole face at the last thought.

In her initial cleaning of Bill's den, she had not found any of her books, dutifully shared with her family over the years. At the time, she'd thought that Susan or her kids carried the books to Oregon with them. Polly had a degree in history though earned her living making handmade pottery. Philip never graduated, and none of the majors he tried were in the humanities. Like Susan, he was suspicious of reading too much. It might cause a rupture in their manic shields.

I need to pick up Abby now, but tomorrow, I think I'll go downtown to that used bookstore to see if, by chance, Susan unloaded them there, she decided.

The next morning she did just that and was actually surprised to find the very book she had hoped for. Her *Crime and Punishment: Murder in England in the Fourteenth Century* sat on the history shelf next to a rough but whole copy of Georges Duby's *The Chivalrous Society.* Nice company I keep.

At first, of course, she couldn't be sure this copy of her book hadn't belonged to a student or even a professor at the local university. But when she opened it to the title page, there was her inscription — *For Bill and Susan, with Love — Judith Chandler.* The words inadequate and formal in spite of the "with Love." Book signings revealed that inscribing books for someone she hardly knew was difficult. But for her family, she found it nearly impossible to think of anything to write especially since she knew they would just put it on a shelf or in a cupboard until she visited. Or sell it off.

It felt strange to buy this book with her name across the front and her inscription lurking inside. But, the college student who checked her out and took her credit card didn't notice that the names were the same. Or didn't care. Jude put the book in her bag as she made her way to the door.

Walking to her car in the next block, she wondered why she had bothered to look for this book and buy it when she did find it. I still have a couple of copies of this in California so why do I need this one? "Am I being sentimental or cynical about a gift to the family?" she scoffed aloud and then remembered she was walking on a public sidewalk.

By the time she had driven back to the house and gathered her two sets of notes onto the used dining table, she felt hungry. The morning's apple only a distant memory. Jude made a sandwich and a small pot of tea and then began to eat and compare the two sets of notes.

I don't get it, she thought. The case seems clear enough. Freddie Sanborn found along the riverbank on the north shore near the bridge, head bashed in, bruises all over his arms and legs. A drunken drifter roused nearby with a bloody baseball bat in his hand. One article summing up the case quoted the District Attorney: "There is no question as to this man's guilt. We have the weapon in his hand, at the scene, and, according to the coroner, within a couple of hours of the boy's death." And the DA proceeded to put the case to bed rather handily. The drifter was sentenced to hang for the murder. The sentence was carried out within the year. So why did Bill write those cryptic notes next to the DA's statement and every other article that quoted the DA's certainty of the evidence? What could Bill possibly have known that the DA's office and the police did not?

Her sandwich gone and the tea grown cold, Jude stood up and stretched. Rufus was poking at the gap under the basement door. That made the hair on the back of Jude's neck prickle.

"Rufus. Cut. That. Out," she scolded. Then she tossed one of his toys into the next room to distract him. It did.

Jude opened the basement door, speaking forcefully to herself. "I can't keep avoiding this damnable, stinking basement. Even if daylight can't penetrate those narrow, dirty basement windows, I can switch the light on in each of the three rooms."

Silently, she mused, I need to check for water leakage and see that the pump is working before the next storm hits tonight. This time of year it can rain hard. I have to be prepared. She talked herself down the stairs, switching on each room's single bulb as she went, and remembering the many hours she had spent with her family huddled in the first room when police or tornado sirens wailed. The summer she turned 12, constant tornado warnings forced the family to retreat to the basement repeatedly.

I kept a laundry basket full of my most valuable possessions so when the sirens went off, I could pick it up, put my goldfish bowl on top, and carry the precarious lot to the basement, she recalled. That spring, it seemed as if we were down here every other day! Okay, the basement did protect us, too. She sighed and went into the second room where the laundry chute emptied into a large, standing wooden crate. The main chute opening in the upstairs hallway outside the three bedrooms down the hall from her parents. Susan used to threaten to stuff her in there if Jude annoyed her.

Ah, she *did* have a dark side, Jude mused. But that had been fully overcome by Susan's late-built, impregnable wall-of-happiness. When did she change? Why? Jude shook off the thought of her sister and walked further into the second room.

In this room, her mother shelved the glass Mason jars full of fruits and vegetables, ready to be consumed during the winter months. Before the grocery stores carried fruit and veg from far beyond the region, from wherever the produce was still growing during the winter months in the Midwest.

I don't remember feeling deprived, Jude thought. I suppose I would now if I couldn't get my pineapple in January or my apples in March. Maybe I've lived in California too long. Focus, Jude, where is that bloody pump?

The dirt floor was slightly sticky but not flooded at all, she noticed, as she went into the third room. The main room of her nightmares.

"Okay, so this room is smelly and the foundation really cracked but mostly solid. Why was this room so terrifying? Only my mother seemed comfortable coming into this part of the basement."

Jude cast her eyes over the detritus on the rocky projections that looked shelf-like but were part of the foundation that had shifted only slightly over the century or so of its life as a house.

What is *this*? she wondered.

An old pie safe nearly stripped of stain, with the punched tin insets looking more punched than they should, leaned against one of the rock support pillars.

"This wasn't here when Mom died. Was it?" she asked the room.

The cupboard looked so fragile that she feared touching it would make it crumble like the untended paper of a medieval manuscript.

Had the basement damp preserved or destroyed it, she wondered. With that thought, she carefully reached out to open one of the two doors.

The knob was damp and clammy to Jude's touch but stayed firm as she pulled the door open. The door creaked and moaned, momentarily unsettling Jude's resolve to investigate. Her historian's instincts urged her on. Damp dirt scarred with mouse prints that might be ancient or brand new covered the shelves inside. The interior smelled moldy, earthy. She couldn't stop herself from thinking of "John Brown's body lies a-mouldering in his grave," a song from her elementary school days. That song always made her skin crawl and helped people her subsequent nightmares.

She started to shut the door again when something in the dank interior glinted in the light of the bare bulb overhead. Against her own better judgment, she reached inside and her hand closed over part of a solid metal object. She gripped it tightly and felt the grit on it. Jude pulled it out of the cabinet and turned toward the grimy basement window that faced west. A slight sliver of late afternoon light fell across the metal box which turned out to be one of those Christmas tins holding cookies or candy and later used by housewives of her mother's era as a gift container for homemade divinity, fudge, or peanut brittle. The lid was stuck tightly to the base. Jude couldn't budge it. That and the sound of her daughter coming in the front door were enough to get Jude out of the basement and back upstairs.

Abby and Rufus were both staring at her as she opened the basement door. "I had to go down to check the pump (which I forgot to do she thought to herself) and found this." She held the tin out and reached for a paper towel to try to wipe the grime from it.

"Mom, that looks nasty."

"This should make it somewhat less nasty," she replied as she wiped it down. Then Jude took a cloth towel, covered the lid, and started to pull along the lip. Finally, with a pop and a rather unpleasant metallic odor wafting up from the interior of the box, the lid gave way. She pulled it off the rest of the way, turned it towel-side down on the counter, and looked inside. Shiny, dusty crumbs. Cookie or candy would be hard to determine. Nothing more.

"Well?" her daughter peered over Jude's shoulder at the dirty box on the counter.

"Nothing. I don't know what I expected," Jude laughed off her hope of the mystery of the scrapbook being revealed in a box of pictures or letters. "I need to get cleaned up so we can try that new restaurant downtown." She smiled earnestly at her daughter, but thought to herself—and be among the living.

Her mood was defiant and deflated at the same time as she went upstairs. Rufus, unimpressed by it all, swished his tail haughtily and followed Abby out of the room.

The restaurant had been a bank throughout Jude's childhood but now was a flossy new gastropub. Microbrewery passe'. Gastropub cool. Amusing herself with this thought and scanning the crowd of diners, Jude followed Abby and the hostess to a table. Abby was gazing around at the clientele more as Jude perused the shiny, laminated menu.

"I'd forgotten how many meat dishes there could be on a Midwestern menu. Oh, wait, this sounds hearty, good, *AND* vegetarian. Cheddar cheese soup made with a German pilsner-style vegetarian beer, hunks of dark brown bread on the side," Jude exclaimed.

Her satisfied smile withered as she glanced up at her daughter's frowning face. "I don't see anything that sounds good, Mother." Abby was flipping the menu from back to front. "The seared scallops might be good, but they can't be fresh!"

Abby's West Coast snobbery reminded her of her own during her first weeks back in this part of the country. She had to laugh, but Abby was not amused by that.

"It's a reasonable assumption, Mother."

"I'm sure they're fine. They have a tasty sounding quinoa burger though. You like quinoa." Jude did her best to pacify her California girl.

"That was my only other choice. Too much meat on this menu."

The carnivorous and conservative habits of the Midwest always conflicted with Jude's propensity to champion the weak, animal or human, too.

At age three, Jude had witnessed the Thanksgiving turkey's beheading, body running, neck wildly spurting blood. After that, she refused to eat meat though her mother cajoled constantly even seeking help from their pediatrician. The pediatrician argued that Jude's willingness to eat vegetables, fruits, and dairy would preserve her health. After that, Jude was never foced to eat meat again.

During visits to her family as an adult, Jude had played down their conflicting philosophies of life in order to keep the peace. But, living here full-time again could destabilize even Jude's resolve toward peace.

Jude and Abby enjoyed their food and each other's company in spite of the meaty menu. Abby was brightening up daily since she met Emily, and being out in the world away from the ghosts of Jude's ancestral home were lifting Jude's spirits.

Yet, Jude's recollections of the constant negotiation demanded of her in maneuvering her family's emotional maze made one nagging thought about her late brother-in-law linger. Did Bill's suicide have anything to do with that scrapbook?

She thought she had stifled that persistent question but then, in a post-book-revision rush, picked up the scrapbook again. Going through it a second time and more methodically, she hoped to discover something that would reveal the answer—an adolescent affair with Freddie Sanborn—in 1968 that would have made an 18-year-old boy anxious and fearful, but surely not as an adult in the 2000s? Several of her gay friends had married women and, sometime much later, come out and left the marriage. But, there was nothing she ever knew or heard about Bill that inclined her to this conclusion. She couldn't help but wonder about the cause.

Bill killed Freddie Sanborn in a fit of teen angst over a girl, found the drifter asleep along the riverbank, and put the bloody bat in his hand? she imagined. I don't remember hearing Bill even raise his voice to her or the kids however exasperating Susan could be. It's true that suicide has no rational explanation, no fault. Not the self-murderer's or his family or friends. No one could say or do anything to stop another person who really wanted to die, could they? she wondered.

Jude felt perplexed and despairing at the same time as one other memory slipped in. She could still see the face of a despondent, Vietnam vet who came to the first group meeting when she was an undergrad TA in a touchy-feely communications course. We did all kinds of (now seemingly) silly exercises to get folks to "get in touch with themselves," she remembered, but the vet remained mostly silent in that first class. We thought it was because he was nearly 20 years older than most of the students, including us TAs. The next week when we met, the professor called us into his office ahead of our group meeting to tell us that this man had committed suicide. My first thought was that I should have sensed his trouble somehow. But that man was a stranger who had not shared anything about himself with us that night. How could we know? Bill was not a stranger. Even though I hadn't seen him for almost a decade, he and I always liked each other, and I believed that he understood why I stopped accepting Susan's invitations to visit, that it had nothing to do with him.

These thoughts had kept Jude quiet as she paid the check, but as they walked out into the cool autumn night, Abby started to talk about the Halloween dance at school and what costumes she and Emily were contemplating. Jude forced herself to pay attention. Abby continued to talk about costumes and the dance during the walk to the car in the chill of late October, but none of that was enough to clear Jude's head from darker thoughts. Though she tried.

"We'd better get home to our lucky black cat, Abby."

Back at the house with Rufus complaining about, well, everything, Abby finally scooped him up and went to bed. Jude stayed downstairs at the table continuing to worry over Bill's motivations.

If Bill had just left a note, she thought. I've wondered about the absence of one. Bill never went out of the house when Susan was gone without leaving her a note. I found notes on scraps of paper, on post-its, scribbled on the edge of an old TV guide. Bill was a note maker. Even in the scrapbook, whatever those brief notes in the margins mean, he thought it important to make them. Bill had a historian's mind, and historians can be obsessed with notes.

"Bill, where's your suicide note?" Her sudden articulation of this thought made her jump up from the kitchen chair she had unconsciously been occupying.

She realized then that she hadn't removed her coat after coming inside some time ago. She did that now and, absentmindedly, started to hang it on the old, oak hall tree that had for decades occupied one corner of the entryway. Sighing, she turned and tossed her coat on a chair and quickly made her way upstairs.

Bill's scrapbook was back in the cabinet in the den. She didn't know exactly why she had put it away separately from her own notes which were shoved into a folder on her desk. One more time through this book, she encouraged herself.

She sat on the overstuffed chair with the scrapbook in hand and slowly looked over each page of articles with Bill's cryptic notes, glaring from the margins. She reached the last of the 12 pages filled with articles when she realized that she had never examined the pages in the rest of the book, assuming they were empty like the thirteenth page. About a third of the way before the end of the bound scrapbook, she found a carefully folded piece of paper wedged between two pages. She was surprised at the steadiness of her hands as she opened the folded paper.

Blank. No writing. Not even a stray pencil mark, she sighed.

She sat a long time in the half-lit room. The lamp next to the chair burned brightly but failed to illumine more than the space around the overstuffed chair. Not a sound came from down the hall where Rufus and Abby slept peacefully, dreaming of mice (Rufus) and dancing (Abby). Jude could hear only her own breath, in and out, in and out.

III

Secrets and Lies

A sharp, rap on the door downstairs brought Jude upright in her bed one morning nearly a month later. Her head stuck in a dream kept her disoriented for a few minutes. It must be a FedEx delivery. She started to get out of bed when the sound of knocking, louder this time, came again. Well, that's not FedEx. They ring or knock once and then are gone like a shot. I'd better go down before whoever it is wakes Abby.

Winter had arrived so the warm-ups she slept in would do for answering the door. What time is it? she wondered, grabbing her phone and starting down the stairs. Too early for deliveries or visitors. Oh, please don't let it be missionaries!

"Rufus, watch it." The cat rushed by her on the first flight of stairs and abruptly stopped, staring out the window there. The knock came a third time. Rufus growled.

When she reached the door, she opened it not a little angry by the intrusion so early in the morning. "Yes." She stared unblinking at the stranger.

The man on her doorstep had dark, wavy hair and a short goatee flecked with gray. "Hi, Susan Franklin?" The man's voice was hesitant.

"No, I'm sorry. Susan has moved away."

"Oh, well…" the man's eyes shifted from Jude's face to his feet and back.

Jude had been an urban dweller long enough to be suspicious of a random man at the door at any time of day. Just because he knew her sister's name didn't mean a thing. He could easily get that information online these days. Her voice did not disguise her hardening attitude.

"Is there a message I can send her?"

The man seemed frustrated now and more unsure than before. He mumbled, "No, thanks," and turned to go down the stairs.

Jude stepped back inside closing the storm door, then the heavy oak one. She flipped the deadbolt. Rufus had watched the exchange from the window on the landing between the first and second flight of stairs that connected the downstairs living area with the bedrooms upstairs. He didn't like people intruding on his house and kept up the low growl. Rufus stayed put until he heard Jude lock the door; then he came flying.

"Rufus, what the heck are you doing?" Jude's mood lifted with the antics of her cat, but she still watched the man walking slowly to a new model, but obviously rental, car parked in the oversized gravel driveway her father had created decades before. "I don't like strange folks coming to the door either, Rufus. Let's forget about the intruder and find some breakfast."

Abby had slept through the knocking and the encounter so Jude didn't mention it to her when she came down for breakfast.

Even though Jude intended to forget the whole incident herself, the stranger's visit left Jude feeling uneasy. After she got back from taking Abby to school, Jude diligently went upstairs to the den to check her email.

The first copyedited chapter of her book would be in the Dropbox folder. The first email read, Jude started right to work on the revisions. Although this activity would have normally absorbed Jude, she couldn't keep focused that day

She took a walk in the cold, late November air, made herself a more elaborate lunch than usual, and then played toss-the-catnip-mouse with Rufus until he was bored. Jude tried to make herself get back to work but realized she was looking forward with more eagerness to Linda's visit in a couple of weeks. It would be a relief to have an adult with whom she could confide all her suspicions and fears, especially after this morning's strange encounter, the only phrase that came to her to describe what had happened.

By 3 o'clock, Jude had finally pulled her mind back to her work. Abby was going to Emily's house after school and then spending the night. Jude knew she needed to finish her response to this first chapter while Abby was away. She wouldn't have to take a break for food until her body, or Rufus, started fussing at her. Three hours later, Rufus started bawling for his dinner. Jude sighed and closed her laptop.

"Yes, Rufus, I know, it's your dinner time." Jude ruffled the cat's fluffy head and headed down the stairs, Rufus running ahead. He froze almost mid-step when he reached the landing. Jude saw someone standing on the porch. The faintest shadow in the setting sun.

"What the hell!"

She was down the steps and at the door before the sound of the knock faded. She turned on the bright porch light to put the intruder off guard a bit. Then she opened the oak door. The man from this morning stood on the other side of the locked storm door. Now that she had opened the main door, she debated briefly how to proceed. She unlocked the storm door and stepped out onto the porch closing the door behind her.

"Susan still doesn't live here."

"I'm sorry. I should have said this morning. It's really Bill Franklin that I'm looking for."

The hair on the back of Jude's neck stood up and a chill swept over her. "Bill Franklin." She repeated the name as if she hadn't heard it correctly.

"Yes." The man shifted his weight from one foot to the other but looked directly at Jude's face this time.

"Are you a friend of Bill's?"

"Not exactly. We've never met actually, well, not that I can recall, but I know him. I mean, I know about, I—" His stuttering speech trailed off.

His stammering made Jude nervous. But it also made her strangely curious because there was something familiar about this man's face.

"Well?" Icy.

The muscles in the man's neck tightened, "I'm Bill's son."

Jude was certain that she heard him wrong this time. "You're who?"

"I'm Bill Franklin's son by his first wife, Carol Ann Sherman."

"Bill's first wife?" The fact that Bill had a wife before Susan was news to her, let alone a son.

"Yes. My mother married Bill Franklin in June of 1969. I was born the next year."

"Where, where were they married? Where's your mother? Where have you been?"

These and more questions scattered Jude's normally rational thought processes into a staccato of rude-sounding inquiries.

"Is Bill here?" the man now seemed firmly rooted to the porch.

"No." Jude wasn't ready to offer anything more to this man who may or may not be Bill's son. Bill's son. The only son of Bill's she'd ever known was Philip, Susan and Bill's oldest. "Listen, this is a bit much for me to take in just now, and I am not willing to invite a stranger into my house without more solid evidence of who you are. Can we meet in town tomorrow?"

"Yes, please. But, I don't know the town very well."

"Where are you staying?"

"At the Holiday Inn Express not far from here."

"Have you seen the Dunkin' Donuts a few blocks east of where you're staying?"

"I can find it."

"I'll meet you there at 10 o'clock tomorrow morning. O.K.?"

"Thank you." His feet disconnected from the concrete porch as he turned quickly, walked down the stairs, and crossed the yard to his car.

Jude watched him until he got in his car and backed out of the driveway. Then she went inside and put the deadbolt on, very glad that Abby was at Emily's.

At 9:55 the next morning, Jude walked into the Dunkin' Donuts. At that time of day, it was mostly students studying or people just picking up donuts at the counter and leaving. The man who claimed to be Bill's son was already sitting in a corner table near one glass window wall. She acknowledged him with a wave and went to the counter. Jude joined him with her tea a few minutes later.

She wasted no time on pleasantries. "I hope you will indulge me and show me some kind of written proof, more than your driver's license, something that will prove you are Bill's son. And, what is *your* name."

"My last name is Sherman. Jim Sherman. I guess my mother wanted no reminders of Bill Franklin's paternity. I thought, well, I thought Bill Franklin would want some more tangible proof than my word." The man handed Jude an envelope that he had pulled from a soft briefcase.

He looked miffed, but Jude didn't care. She needed official documents. She also thought she would be able to spot anything phony after her years in the archives with documents of every kind. Even in medieval

Europe and certainly in academic circles, forgeries happened.

Jude took her time studying the papers he had given her. First, a birth certificate—a baby boy born to Carol Ann Sherman Franklin, mother and William J. Franklin, father. The document had the State seal and a date in February 1970, a month shy of nine months from June of the year before, the date he had given her yesterday for his parents' marriage. The birth certificate was genuine. But where was his current proof of identification? she wondered. An authentic birth certificate could be fabricated these days. Maybe this guy had read about Bill's death and was looking for inheritance or insurance money.

Jude narrowed her eyes and looked up at the man across from her. According to the certificate, he should be only a year younger than Jude, but he looked older. He shifted uneasily as she continued to stare at his face. After a minute more, she looked down at the envelope and pulled out a picture.

A young man and woman smiling with a baby in her arms greeted her.

Shit. That is definitely Bill, she thought.

The Bill Franklin she remembered had been tired-looking, older than his years the last time she had seen him. If not for going through his senior annual, she might be skeptical that this young man smiling in the photo was Bill at all. She placed the photo beside the birth certificate and pulled out another piece of paper. It was a letter dated June 23, 1970. Four months after the birth certificate declaring a son was born to Bill and Carol Ann.

Dear Carol Ann,

Please come back home. I'm sorrier than you can know about my harsh words. But, you were crying and then the baby started crying. I couldn't get you to listen. When you locked yourself and Jimmy in the bedroom, remember, I pleaded with you. Told you how much I loved you and him. But then you started screaming, saying that I had only married you because you were pregnant. That if I really loved you, I would quit school and go back East with you to your folks. You know I only have one more semester to go for my teaching credentials. If I quit now, I'll have to apply to another school which means waiting longer and maybe not getting into the same kind of program at all. Surely, you understand that would take more time and more money, money we don't have ourselves. Carol Ann, please, just come back, and let me finish school. Then, if you want, we can see about going back East to be near your mom and dad. Please, Carol Ann. I want to be with Jimmy and you.

 Bill

Jude read the letter over twice. Still, she considered, this only proved that Bill had been married before Susan and had a son. It did not prove that this man *was* that son. She told him as much.

But even as she told him that she still needed proof, something the man did surprised Jude. The man frowned at that moment in a way that reminded her of Bill.

Could he really be Bill's son? A son Bill never revealed, a son he never saw beyond infancy? She thought this Jim Sherman could hear her thoughts.

"I don't know what else I can show you to prove that I am his son. Let me talk to Bill. Where is he anyway?"

"Bill's dead." Jude didn't intend to blurt it out like that but felt some relief at having done so.

"What? What do you mean he's dead?" his face visibly sagging, his hand went to his forehead covering his eyes. When he took his hand away a few minutes later, their shine told her the truth.

"I'm sorry to be so blunt."

"How did he die? When?"

"He...died this past summer. June." Jude couldn't bring herself to tell him Bill committed suicide.

"I can't believe I missed him by just a few months." Jim Sherman was visibly shaken by the news so Jude went to the counter for a cup of strong, black tea with lots of sugar.

"Here, drink this, slowly. It's hot." She was a firm believer in black tea with multiple teaspoons of sugar as a remedy for shock or distress.

She watched Jim sip the tea as they sat in silence both lost in their own erratic thoughts. After fifteen minutes, Jude asked, "Does your mother know you're here?"

"She died last year. I found the letter and birth certificate in an old metal box that belonged to her father. I had never looked in it before. She had always said it was just bits of Grandfather's junk that she had to go through some time. Apparently, she forgot about it when she got sick. I found it when I was cleaning out her house after she died. Since then, I've been searching for Bill. I guess I didn't move fast enough."

Jude felt for him but didn't quite know what to say now. She stood up, "I need to get back to my house. The house and the land around it belonged to Susan and my maternal grandparents, then to my parents, and finally Susan and me. When Bill died, I bought Susan out, but I actually live and work in the Bay Area in California. I'm a history professor on sabbatical this year." Jude wasn't sure why she had told him so much or why she still neglected to tell him her name. "Listen, if you aren't leaving town today, you can call me later at this number." She wrote down her cell number on a napkin and slid it across the table.

"O.K." The lines on his face deepened as his hand closed over the napkin.

"Good-bye, Jim."

Jude walked out into the cold blue of a November day.

IV
Revelations

Her cell rang just as Jude hit "Send" on the email to her publisher with the first chapter attached. She had to pull herself back from editing mode and search for her phone. Rufus had apparently been lying on it. When she turned toward the sound, she saw the cat jump up indignantly away from the vibrating, ringing beast beneath him. She smiled and reached for her phone.

"Hello," Jude said gaily expecting her friend Linda who was due in next week.

"Hello," the voice, deep and masculine was not Linda's. "It's Jim. Jim Sherman. You said I could call you."

"Oh, yes. Of course. How are you today?" Gaiety gone, Jude thought her question sounded ridiculous given the bomb she had dropped on him just before walking away the day before.

"Fine. Could we meet for lunch or something?" his voice strained, tense.

"Yes, no problem. Let's see. There's a good Chinese place on the same street as your hotel. Have you seen it?" Jude moderated her nervousness by focusing on a visual of the street.

"I've seen it. When, what time would work for you?"

"In an hour?"

"See you then."

Jude tapped the red off button and sat quietly, still holding the phone until Rufus jumped in her lap tossing his fluffy tail across her nose.

Startled, Jude moved just enough to send the cat, indignant, back to the floor. "Sorry, Rufus."

The cat flounced off in a huff, and Jude pulled herself up from the chair. She was stiff. She'd been sitting in that cheap office chair working at her computer since Abby went to school about three hours ago. She stood still a moment more before heading to the bathroom for a shower.

I need to clear my head before I meet this guy again. Jim. Bill's son. But, what can I do for him now?

Again, Jim had arrived earlier than Jude and taken a table in a far corner of the restaurant. She walked over in response to his raised hand, unwittingly ignoring the hostess starting to ask her the usual question.

Jim actually stood up as she came to the table to sit down.

Now, that's an old-fashioned bit of etiquette I don't miss, Jude thought as she smiled weakly.

She sat down.

Jim Sherman resumed his seat and stammered, "Thank you for coming. I—" The waiter came over just at that moment.

Jude didn't need a menu as she had frequented this place for the last few months.

They ordered quickly and then Jim tried again. "I hope you don't mind if I ask you a few questions about, about my, I mean about Bill Franklin."

"No. But, you should know that I haven't been around much for the last 20 years. I knew Bill, but I wouldn't say I knew him well. He was my sister's husband. They were quite a bit older than I, married when I was only a child. I have memories of him as a kind, older brother type from those early years, but from college on I lived on the West Coast. I came home a couple of times a year and then not at all for the last ten years. After my parents had both passed away," she added as if that summed up the whole of her relationship with Bill.

"Oh, well. You knew him though. And he was kind?"

She felt sorry for Sherman but wasn't sure what she could tell him that might help him deal with whatever emotional roller coaster he had boarded.

"He was. Bill taught history at the high school here even before he and my sister were married until, until he died last summer." She didn't want to reveal the cause of her brother-in-law's death just yet. Not until she could be sure this guy wasn't out for something other than personal closure.

"That's why I, uh…I'm a network administrator at the state geological survey. In Washington, the state, not D.C."

"Oh, you don't live back East somewhere? The letter you showed me yesterday said that your mother's parents lived on the East Coast." Jude challenged, narrowing her eyes much as she did when confronting a student lying about why they missed the exam.

He had been holding his breath, now exhaling audibly, "They did. She did, but I, my job was in Seattle.

"So, what were you going to say—That's why…what?" Jude pressed him.

"You said that Bill did go on to be a teacher. That has to be why my mother put up such a fight against my taking a teaching degree. It makes sense now, well, as much sense as she ever made."

The last part of that statement intrigued Jude more than the first.

Was this woman, Carol Ann, a bit off? Jude wondered. Bill professed his love for her, but was it more to keep his son with him? Bill never failed, after all, to put Susan and the kids first, especially the kids. That's what seems so awful in their response to his death. Bill did everything for them and then, when he died, they did nothing for him.

Jude realized she had been silent, caught up in her own thoughts too long. Jim was staring at her anxiously when she focused on him again.

"Well, sure. She had unpleasant memories of…" Jude trailed off not quite sure what Carol Ann's unpleasant memories might have been.

"Mom said that teaching stole time and money from the family. Since my grandparents had set aside my college fund, I didn't feel I could argue with her about it. Well, I was tired of trying so I finally got her to compromise. I went into computer programming and networking, and she approved once she realized how many jobs were out there and how much money I could make."

Judging by the weary look on Jim's face, this was not the only argument with his mother he had lost. Jude was softening some toward him but still kept her guard up.

"So, what do you want to know about Bill besides his profession? I can tell you he was a faithful husband and excellent father." She realized the potential pain that last bit might cause, only too late.

No reaction.

"The letter I showed you seemed to indicate that he cared about me and my mother. Just not enough to come after us. Or change his mind about teaching."

Jude suddenly felt protective of her dead brother-in-law. "Whatever happened between your mother and father had nothing to do with you, Jim. Bill was devoted to his two children, my nephew and niece. And he was a damned good teacher, winning several teaching awards over the years."

"Sorry, I didn't mean—I wouldn't know, not really. Only what my mother told me. She said that he didn't care about us and so she went back East to her parents, eventually divorced him, and never remarried. I had no reason not to believe her until I found that letter. Then, I wondered."

Jude started to speak just as the waiter came up with their orders. Each remained silent, stuck in their own heads, as they opened chopsticks and began to eat.

Finally, Jude admitted, "I didn't mean to sound defensive, but Bill was a good guy. I'm sorry about what happened between Bill and your mom, but neither of us really knows about that and shouldn't speculate." Though Jude was starting to do just that in her head.

"Of course. Yes, you're right. My mother wasn't an easy woman so I chose a job far enough away to keep some distance between us. I visited her infrequently with one excuse or another, and she only came to see me once. We never enjoyed our visits. Either of us. That and my job had kept me away for years. I felt guilty that I didn't visit more. Don't get me wrong, I did go back to tend her in her final illness, and I did grieve for my mother after her death. Just not in the way I thought I should."

"I understand, having spent most of my adult life away from my family. Even though I loved my parents, our way of being in the world was vastly different. I used to think I was adopted because I was not like anyone in my family." Jude hadn't meant to be so forthcoming, so personal, but this man's plight and obvious pain was starting to have an effect on her. "Jim, when do you have to go back to Seattle?" Jude scooped up rice and veg and popped it in her mouth, hoping he would be expansive in his reply.

"I took a week of vacation hoping to find Bill and have some time with him. To hear his side of things. I only have three days left. I struggled awhile once I arrived. I told myself I was crazy to do this at all. I had to talk myself back into, not confronting Bill, but just going to see him. That took a while."

"I imagine that would be hard." She still wasn't sure about him really. "I should be getting back to the house before—" Jude started to mention Abby but thought better of it.

"I've taken up enough of your time. I'm grateful." Jim stammered again and beckoned the waiter.

Neither of them spoke until they were at the door.

"Have a good flight back to Seattle, Jim. I'm sorry I couldn't be more help." Jude felt drained for some reason.

Why am I being so cautious, so dismissive now, she wondered.

As she looked at Jim's dejected face before he turned away, she thought about Bill. Should she tell his son how he died? Should she tell him that she thinks Bill had a deeper secret even than his son's existence?

"Jim, wait," Jude called to his back just before he stepped off the walkway next to the restaurant.

When he turned, Jude suddenly wasn't sure what she wanted to say next. "We could get together again before you go if you want. You might even come to the house tomorrow evening?" The last did sound more like a question than an invitation, but Jim nodded agreement. "I'll call you later," Jude had to raise her voice over a diesel dually coming between them.

Then, they both continued in opposite directions toward their cars.

Jude suddenly thought her wits must have left her. Why am I keeping this going? And why isn't it Susan who has to deal with this? Oh, yeah, I can see that ever working out. I wish I could tell Jim how fortunate he is that Susan *wasn't* at the house when he came. She would have freaked out completely and probably even called the police on him, or threatened to.

Abby announced just before her bedtime that she would be going to Emily's to spend the night tomorrow night. Taken aback by the declarative rather than the interrogative, Jude started to protest that Abby had just spent last Friday night at Emily's so why not have Emily here, when Jude remembered what she had set in motion—Jim Sherman coming to dinner tomorrow night.

"O.K. fine," Jude said thinking that would keep Abby safely out of the way.

Abby picked up the cat and danced happily off to her bedroom. Jude sat a while longer at the table in the kitchen before heading upstairs herself. She checked the front door lock and turned off the lights downstairs, wondering what exactly she would tell Jim Sherman tomorrow night.

Should I really bring him to my house, she questioned? He *is* a stranger even if he *is* Bill's son. If his mother was unhinged, maybe he is, too.

Jude kept plaguing herself with these kinds of thoughts as she washed her face and brushed her teeth. But, just as she was about to crawl into bed, she stopped, turned, and walked into the den.

Since the two rooms had, during her grandparents' day, been an apartment for young student couples, the bank of cabinets on the wall also had a small countertop and sink with a couple of drawers below the sink. Beneath these were three more cabinets. Jude had placed the annual, scrapbook, and a folder with her notes into the larger of the two drawers.

"I need to look at all this again." Jude said aloud to herself though she lowered her voice on the last three words. She did not want to wake Abby or get Rufus stirred up.

Hearing her lone voice in that room, she again felt the goosebumps rising on her arms as she had her first night alone there.

If Bill's ghost exists it must be flitting wildly about now with the prospect of Jim coming and me still digging through his scrapbook, she thought as she pulled the materials from the drawer.

She brought all the documents to her small desk in the corner by the window and turned the switch on her desk lamp. She started to flip slowly through the scrapbook with her black and white composition notebook (her preferred type for research) on the right and the high school annual on the left. When she came to the clipping with the picture of the three boys, she opened the annual to the page she had flagged for the photograph of the All-Americans, Bill, her brother Robbie, and Freddie Sanborn, their senior year. Then Jude turned the pages of her notebook until she came to the notes she had taken on the trial for the day that clipping's photo was taken.

Bill had written "Liars" in the margin next to the article in his scrapbook. Jude had initially thought that he was talking about the report of the prosecution's examinations of witnesses and their closing argument that day. But her own notes on the trial records made her wonder if Bill had been referring to these at all.

What if, what if he meant that these boys, including himself, were the liars, she conjectured? She glanced at her notes which contained two other reporters' versions of that day. Nothing in those or the article's account confirmed either interpretation.

Out of the darkness on the floor, Rufus leaped up on her desk nearly knocking the lot off onto the floor.

"Rufus."

Too loud. Don't wake Abby, Jude scolded herself silently. Now whispering, she fussed at the cat and shooed him off her desk. Insulted, Rufus tossed his tail in the air and sauntered into her room.

He'll be in the middle of my bed now making every effort to be in my way so he can act offended when I move him, she knew.

But the cat had helped dispel the trance she had been putting herself into staring at first one, then the other picture, and comparing Bill's notes with her notes, with the article. She sighed, turned out her desk lamp, and went to bed.

But she couldn't sleep. Her brain would not be silent.

In the morning, Jude was distracted by getting Abby off to school with the added gear for her overnight at Emily's. Emily picked up Abby so Jude stayed in, planning her day of preparations for the evening with Jim Sherman.

What am I going to say to him? Should I tell him that Bill committed suicide? Jude visibly started with that thought.

"Wait a minute, Rufus," she said aloud as the cat strutted into the room. "Why didn't Jim Sherman know that Bill was dead *and* that it was suicide. After all, he has the technical skills to get as much as possible out of an internet search about his father. How else did he track him down to this house in Bill's hometown? How hard could that have been? And wouldn't articles about Bill's suicide have been readily available in any name search?" Jude stood up as if to have a confrontation with someone and went purposefully to her computer upstairs. Jude barked, "Let's see what we can find online about Bill Franklin." Rufus agreed.

But she would be immediately disappointed when she started searching for "William J. Franklin obituary." The first result was the legacy.com obituary notice of Bill's death, published by the mortuary and the local paper:

William J. "Bill" Franklin, 68, of Lawson died on Monday, June 23. Bill taught history at Lawson High School for 45 years before he retired this year. His wife, Susan, of the home, and his children, Philip and Polly, of Corvallis, Oregon survive.

Seriously, that's it? Jude thought. I shouldn't be surprised. Susan certainly wasn't about to publish to the world the fact that he committed suicide. Or apparently anything else about him—his university degrees, his teaching awards or any of his life beyond Susan and their kids. Still, this should have come up in Jim Sherman's search for his father.

Jude frowned and stared at the results of her own search.

So, how *did* Jim Sherman find out where Bill and Susan lived but not that Bill had died? Jim had both their names. Knew his father was married again. "Maybe…" As the word faded in the air, she typed her brother-in-law's name into the search engine. As with every name search on the internet, the results started with several so-called White Pages sites.

Okay, she mused, that would give him the address if he had known Bill's home state. Did he? I definitely have a few more questions for Jim Sherman.

Not a little exasperated, Jude turned to chores for the day. She cleaned up around the house, strewn with the leavings of a teenager and a distracted academic. Jude also had to make a grocery store run so she could make a pot of lentil soup and some cornbread.

Simple soup and bread is always good in winter and comforting without commitment, she reasoned. Jude still doubted the wisdom of her invitation to this suspect stranger to continue a conversation that was more than a little unsettling. And to do it in her own home.

Why not a restaurant? she wondered, as she chopped the vegetables for the soup.

Rufus did not find her domestic activities soothing since they disturbed his usual, lazy routine. He wailed now at her feet.

"It's not your dinner time yet, Rufus," she admonished as she did her best not to step on the cat as he impeded her movement from stove to counter and back. "Okay, mister, I'll feed you so that you can be asleep before company comes."

The word, "company," spoken aloud sent her tumbling back to a childhood memory of one of the rhymes her grandmother had taught her and that she had dutifully recited at some function her mother took her to when Jude was about eight:

I wish that I were company instead of living here.
  You wouldn't say now run and play or Mother's busy, dear.
  Or gracious wash your face and hands, the child's a sight to see.
  You're always good to company but never good to me.

"Wow, I can't believe I remembered even that much of that old nursery rhyme, Rufus," Jude said.

Rufus ignored her as he was greedily eating his crunchies nearby.

Her thoughts continued silently. So "company" referred to guests, people outside the family who received special treatment. Well, nothing special happening for Jim Sherman tonight, except perhaps some revelations of an uncomfortable kind. My sympathies got the better of me yesterday when I invited him here for tonight.

"I'll need to be on my guard," she spoke aloud hearing her mother's skepticism of strangers in her own voice.

An hour later, Jude was seated across her kitchen table from Jim Sherman, who sat nervously and somehow apologetically in his chair.

"Thank you so much for the delicious meal," Jim smiled slightly as he spoke. "I haven't had homemade soup or amazing bread like that since my grandmother died. Unfortunately, I never learned to cook because my mother refused to let Grandmother teach me, and I never had the nerve on my own. I eat out a lot in Seattle." He didn't seem to be able to make eye contact with Jude as he spoke.

"I'm glad you enjoyed it. I started cooking, if you could call it that, before I could reach the counter. My mother was pretty indulgent in that way but also thought all girls should be able to cook a meal. I liked cooking and baking so the gender bias didn't bother me then or later," Jude's smile was not unpleasant, but it wasn't particularly engaging either.

"This is a great old house," Jim expanded a bit not apparently noticing the absence of warmth in Jude's voice or her rather stiff posture.

"I never liked this house. Well, I shouldn't say that. I just felt more comfortable outside than in when I was growing up here, even when my grandmother was still alive." Jude noted sardonically that their conversation had suddenly descended into a kind of homage to grandmothers.

But she distracted him with a question. "So, Jim, how did you locate Bill and Susan?"

Clearly, though he should have expected this, he wasn't ready, thinking they were still making polite, though inane conversation. "Internet search" was all he said.

"Obviously, but in searching for a person by name, we always get a long list of useless sites—actors, politicians, realtors, self-help gurus, the 1940 census data, White Pages. An endless parade of the same names. How did you know which one of these was your Bill Franklin?" Jude had no trouble making eye contact even when the eyes across from her were trying to avoid it.

"I didn't for a long time. As I told you, my mother kept her secrets to the grave. It was my grandfather's old '30s-era metal box that revealed enough to make the connections I needed to pin down which Bill Franklin was my father," he shifted uneasily.

Clearly, Jim Sherman wanted simultaneously to stop the interrogation and reveal what he could. He sighed, stood up, and walked into the entryway. Jude pushed her chair back from the table, making a sharp scraping sound on the wood floor.

Sherman flinched visibly and stopped but only for a few seconds before resuming his path to the chair where his overcoat lay. Jude narrowed her eyes at his reaction as she watched him reach into the inside pocket of his coat. He pulled out the same envelope Jude had seen on their first encounter. His hand reached inside the envelope withdrawing a single sheet of paper. He handed it to Jude.

"You didn't look at this when I gave you the envelope perhaps because you were satisfied with the other documents."

Jude noticed a change in his eyes as she took the paper. It was a photograph of three boys looking down as if in prayer.

"I know this photo. It was in Bill's senior yearbook," she poked her finger at the picture as she identified each boy. "That's Bill. Next to him here, my brother, Robbie, and on Bill's other side, Freddie Sanborn. The only one I ever knew was Bill. My brother was killed in Vietnam the year before I was born."

She held the sheet of paper tightly and continued to stare at the boys' faces, especially Bill's and her brother's.

"I'm sorry. I had no idea that was your brother. I wouldn't have known your last name. I don't actually know your first name."

It sounded like a criticism, but Jude felt no guilt at her reticence. Still, she thought she should give him her name.

"Yes, well, my name is Judith Chandler. I guess yearbook photos show up in an internet search, too." That would explain his knowing that Bill Franklin grew up here, she thought.

Still, her unease increased.

"So, you didn't know any of the three? Just Bill?" Jim suddenly had no problem making eye contact with Jude until she had to look away.

"No. As I said, I didn't know them. Why?" she was curious now.

Why would he be interested in the other two boys in the picture?

"Oh, well, I thought I'd look them up maybe before I left to see what they know about my...father, if they still lived in town."

His face seemed different to Jude who hadn't missed the pause in his last sentence.

"I can't tell you anything else. I have been here so infrequently since I left for college and no one in my family ever wanted to talk about Robbie."

Not even Bill. Odd, if not for the fact that Freddie Sanborn had been murdered and Bill obsessed by it, Jude thought as she stood up to clear the table. She took the dishes and set them in the old, farm-style sink. As she did, the hairs on the back of her neck rose. She nearly fell whirling around.

"Are you alright," Jim's face showed more humor than concern.

Why was that?

"Sure. Yes. Just thought I heard...my cat." The excuse sounded as lame as her voice.

She made an effort to recover her aplomb and her backbone. "Listen, Jim. I'm sorry I couldn't be more help, but I need to do some work tonight before I sleep." Her stance was more defiant than conciliatory.

He got up and went into the entry hall for his coat.

"Of course. Thank you for dinner and the conversation. It was… helpful." He shrugged his coat on as he spoke, and they both moved toward the front door.

"Take care," was all she could manage before nearly shutting him in the door as he stepped onto the porch.

She watched him. Jim Sherman was not a man in a hurry. He walked slowly, deliberately down the steps making his way to the driveway where his rental car waited. When he reached it, Jude turned off the porch light. She had locked the door as soon as she closed it.

She heard Rufus's low, throaty growl when she stepped away from the door and walked into the living room to mount the stairs to the den. Rufus had taken up his favorite place for spying at the landing window and was still watching as the lights of the car swept up over the bare spirea bushes and splashed down onto the street. When the car drove away, Rufus turned toward Jude and snorted.

"I couldn't agree more, Rufus. He was really giving me the creeps. But why?" Jude stepped slowly from stair to stair as if measuring each step's depth and height with her feet.

"High time I searched for Jim Sherman *and* Freddie Sanborn, don't you think, Ruf?"

The cat walked past Jude's room and down the hall to sleep in Abby's bed and bemoan her absence.

V

More Secrets and Lies

After about thirty minutes, Jude's head started to hurt. She pinched the bridge of her nose with her thumb and forefinger and realized as she opened her eyes that the only light on upstairs was the small lamp on her desk. She had been straining her eyes, scanning results lists and one or two documents.

"I'll give it five more minutes; then I'm crashing." Goosebumps broke out over her neck, back, and arms as her voice broke the silence of the dark, November night.

I'm letting this all get to me far beyond its importance in my own life. What the hell!

But even as she said this to herself, she was scanning images that had come up for James Sherman. None resembled the man who had been in her house that night.

She squinted at a grainy, yearbook photograph in gaudy colors. "Really?" she expelled the word in a heavy breath. "Another yearbook photo."

She shook her head but decided to try to maximize the view. A row of faces stared out at her with the name printed under each photograph. Two boys' pictures side by side stopped her: James Sherman and Nathan Sanborn.

"What the—?" her voice was more shriek than shout and Rufus came flying down the hallway. "Sorry, Rufus, but this is too weird."

She pointed at one of the boys whose teenage face looked out at her. "This is not the boy/man who was here tonight calling himself Jim Sherman. He has to be this one, Nathan Sanborn. Oh, Sanborn. Where? When?"

Jude could tell by the hairstyles especially that these kids had been in high school in the late 1990s, several years behind her.

"Where was this? Cleveland, Ohio? Is this guy related to Freddie Sanborn somehow? And, if so, how? And how did he end up in high school in Ohio? And why would he call himself Jim Sherman and be looking for my brother-in-law?"

Jude's brain was wide awake now and firing furiously but in fits and starts. She kept searching online but now for Nathan Sanborn, Ohio. That search revealed only the same yearbook page from the late 1990s. No other photos. No images that would help her find the connections she sought. She grabbed the notebook she'd been using and began to write a series of questions:

Nathan Sanborn, 17 in 1997, how related to Freddie Sanborn, 17 in 1968?

Jim Sherman, 18 in 1997, how related to Bill Franklin, 18 in 1968, if at all?

The birth certificate with embossed, notarized state seal a forgery or stolen document?

The letter from Bill Franklin to "Carol Ann," in what might be Bill's handwriting, but—check the scrapbook against the letter.

The photo from Bill's yearbook was the same as in the original yearbook. Yet, that could easily be copied or printed off the internet. But why?

The Sanborns. What happened to the family after Freddie was killed? Local newspaper archives?

Biggest question. What does this guy, Nathan Sanborn, want from Bill Franklin? And why is he calling himself Jim Sherman?

In the morning, Abby came home ready to take Jude up on a promised shopping trip. That distracted Jude for several hours from the nightmares of Shermans and Sanborns that had disturbed her sleep. Then, Abby and her friend, Emily, were off again to study for another chemistry test and have dinner at Emily's.

"Be home by 9, Abby," Jude called at her daughter's back as the teenager ran across the yard to Emily's car in the driveway.

Now, I have several more hours to search for the Sanborns, she mused.

Jude hurried up the stairs to her room and pulled out Bill's scrapbook to see if she missed anything in the articles or photos attached to them. Nothing new there. Then, she began a search in the local newspaper's archives. A search for Freddie Sanborn revealed all the articles in Bill's scrapbook plus one other. Why didn't Bill include this article with a picture of Freddie's parents and, is that a younger brother? The caption read, "Samuel Sanborn with wife, Jean, and son, Danny at the trial." The article was short and spoke mostly of the grief-stricken family's daily attendance at the trial.

Maybe Bill couldn't bear to see those faces even tucked away in his scrapbook, she thought.

The next result from the newspaper's archives was Freddie Sanborn's obituary notice, printed in the paper two days after his murder. This listed all of Freddie's youthful accomplishments along with the names of the surviving parents, the brother, and the grandparents in Ohio.

"The family must have moved back to Ohio, Rufus," the cat, sleeping in the comfy chair nearby, opened one eye as she spoke.

Jude quickly searched for Ohio newspaper archives. Images popped up first. One was another yearbook photo, this time of Daniel Sanborn, a senior at a high school in Cleveland, Ohio.

Now we're getting somewhere, she thought, as she went to the next item on the list, "Daniel Sanborn, Realtor, Cleveland, Ohio."

Finally, the last link promised something even more informative: "Nathan Sanborn, son of Daniel…" As the link opened up, the face of her visitor appeared in an article from a Cincinnati newspaper. Nathan Sanborn had been hired as the new head of the State Geological Survey's technology unit. "So, he wasn't lying about everything. He does work as a Network Administrator, but not in Seattle. Dammit."

Jude jumped more than stood up out of her chair which rolled back on the hardwood floor and scared Rufus out of his sleep.

"Sorry, Rufus, but I have to get the truth, once and for all!"

At the Holiday Inn Express, Jude walked in half angry, half tentative. Could this guy be dangerous? she wondered, as she continued through the doors and up to the reception desk.

The clerk's pasteboard smile was unpleasant, "Can I help you?"

"Yes, is Jim," what name is he using here? "Is Nathan Sanborn or Jim Sherman staying here?" she gave her own unconvincing version of a smile.

The clerk seemed unfazed by Jude's stumble and checked her computer. "Nathan Sanborn is registered. May I call his room and give him your name?"

Oh, right, Jude thought. She won't just tell me what room he's in. "Yes, thanks. Judith Chandler." She wondered if he would see her or if he was even in. Where else would he be?

The clerk hung up the phone, "He'll be right down."

Nathan Sanborn walked into the lobby a few minutes later, frowning and not a little agitated, "How did you know my real name?"

His expression remained as it had been but he motioned her toward the empty breakfast area. She followed him.

"I am a scholar, though usually my research involves people dead hundreds of years rather than a few decades," Jude was defensive and a bit angry herself. "Why weren't you up front about who you were from the start? Why lie?"

"I shouldn't have. But, it's complicated," Nathan shifted and gestured that they should sit down at a table in the far corner.

"I knew Jim Sherman back in high school. My family's connection to this town wasn't known then. That had come up only recently when Sherman had business in Cleveland. He called me, and we went out for a drink. His mother had died a few months before, and Sherman started telling me that he had finally found out who his father was. I remembered him moaning over his daddy issues even in high school, especially with any alcohol in him. He wanted to find his dad, Bill Franklin, but had promised his mother he would never try. Even in death, she controlled him. Sherman had the documents with him. Meeting him at this point in his life was sheer coincidence, but he had made me curious. I offered to help, and he gave me the documents. Obviously, I did that for my own purposes. I called my dad to find out what he could tell me about Bill Franklin, if anything. He had quite a lot to say."

"What did he tell you?" she prodded.

"Dad said that his older brother, Freddie, had been murdered by a drifter in their hometown the month after he graduated from high school. He had never told me this before. Apparently, the trial had caused a local sensation at the time, and his parents couldn't stand the morbid attention. They moved to Cleveland a month or two after the trial ended, trying to forget it all. My dad was about fifteen or sixteen at the time and had some serious trouble dealing with his brother's death and their move away from all his friends. After college, he married my mom, and, when we kids came along, he put all that behind him. Until I made him think about it again. One thing he said really struck me. One of Dad's friends thought that the boys, Bill and your brother, were lying. No one had questioned their story at the time, and my dad's friend liked to exaggerate and outright lie if it made a good story so Dad had ignored his rantings. But when I pushed him, he admitted to some of his own misgivings about the truth of his brother's death that his friend's assertions had aroused. These bothered him for years." Nathan's frown remained, but his agitation was gone.

Jude wanted to tell him about her discoveries, but his initial subterfuge prevented her. "Still, my question is, why did you come here and lie about who you were, especially after I told you Bill was dead?"

"It felt safer somehow. If Bill Franklin thought I was his long lost son, he might be more forthcoming about other aspects of his early life. He might reveal something that substantiated the other kid's claims. But, when you told me he was dead, I had already shown you the documents and so felt trapped as Jim Sherman."

Jude glared then softened her look at the Jim Imposter, wondering what she should say.

"Look, Jim, Nathan, I don't know anything more about my brother's or my brother-in-law's teen years than you do. They're both dead, so we can't ask them. Nothing more can be said or done. Right?"

Nathan Sanborn shifted in the uncomfortable chair, no longer challenging or aggressive in any way. "You're right. Of course, you're right. I just thought that I might be able to find out something coming here in the town where Dad's brother died."

Although Jude felt for him, she still couldn't bring herself to reveal what she had found in her brother-in-law's old scrapbook. Who would be helped or hurt by such information? she thought.

She stood up and looked down at the clearly dejected face of Nathan Sanborn, "Goodbye, Mr. Sanborn. Have a safe trip back to Ohio."

He said nothing in reply so Jude turned and walked to the door. The cold air hit her like a slap, and she almost went back inside.

Maybe I should give him that damned scrapbook. Leave that puzzle with him so I can get back to my life with my daughter. After all, she fumed to herself, I have to make some decisions of my own before my leave is over about what to do with that bloody house.

She beeped her car door open and slipped behind the wheel, grabbing it as if she had just slammed on the brakes in full rush hour traffic. Then, she sighed and kept expelling air until she could feel it in the muscles of her abdomen.

"Breathe in. Breathe out, Jude," she told herself and did so once, twice, three times before she started the car and drove home.

By the time Abby came home at 9PM sharp, Jude could sit quietly listening to her daughter talk about her evening at Emily's where Emily's dad had made them a "fabulous" pizza before they went off to study.

"What did you do, Mom? Did you eat?" Abby quizzed with a tiny wrinkle of concern, exactly like her mother's.

"Yes, my sweet girl. I had—" Jude frantically racked her brain to remember what leftover she might have eaten earlier, "the rest of the lentil soup I fixed the other night."

Jude answered the second question, hoping to divert her daughter's attention from the absence of an answer to the first one. It worked.

"Good. I'm taking Ruf and going to bed. Chem test tomorrow in first period." Abby scooped up the cat and walked innocently, happily off to her room.

Jude watched the retreating figure of her daughter and smiled. Then, suddenly, she frowned and realized the horror of losing a child, especially the way the Sanborns had lost their oldest son. She felt for Freddie Sanborn's parents and realized how hard that had to be on the little brother, Nathan's father. Then she thought of her own parents' loss. Neither of these boys' remaining family had wanted to talk about their lost sons and brothers.

My parents kept that picture on the wall with Susan's and then mine but never talked about Robbie. Susan never said a word to her about their lost brother. Was that what made her so mean to me? And eventually to contrive a fiction of eternal sunshine for herself?

Jude stared fixedly at the floor until Rufus came squalling down the stairs. The sound made Jude jump, but it also roused her from the darkness in her head. She picked up the fussing cat to quiet him as she made her way upstairs.

When Jude sat down at her computer to revise the proof of one of her chapters the next day, her hands were shaking from more than sufficient quantities of hot, black tea with sugar that she imbibed that morning to dispel her fitful dreams.

I should eat something substantial, she thought, and then ignored herself as she went to her work. She reached for some tea biscuits she kept on her desk and absently nibbled one. An hour later, she sent the chapter off and walked rather distractedly down the stairs to the kitchen.

"What should I do, Rufus?" she asked the cat as if he would have the solution to her quandary.

Rufus just flounced along to sniff at the basement door again. A knock on her door shook her visibly, and the cat took off for the landing on the stairs.

Jude went to the door prepared for a fight, but when she glanced at the side window, she saw a woman at the door.

"Yes, can I help you?" Jude was not one for pleasantries, especially at this particular moment.

"Hello, have you been saved?" the intruder asked with that insipid look all those peddling Jesus door-to-door seem to have.

"Yes, thanks." Jude closed the door in the woman's face and went back to making her cheese sandwich.

"Fucking annoying, do-gooders that do-naught!" Jude swore angrily even though the real cause was the Sanborn/Sherman business rather than the evangelist at the door. That woman had just been the straw.

VI
The End?

"Mom!" Abby's high-pitched exclamation and sudden appearance in the doorway of Bill's old den shook Jude out of her reverie over Bill's scrapbook which lay seemingly unattended in her lap.

"What is it, sweetheart? Something happen? Rufus?" Jude scrambled out of Bill's hazy past to return to her present.

"I've just been calling you for five minutes and had to practically scream to get your attention." Abby stood arms akimbo in the doorway with Rufus at her feet glaring at Jude.

"Well, is something wrong?" Jude's patience was thinning.

"No," Abby all nonchalance now. "I just wanted to know if I could fix dinner for us."

"Of course. What did you have in mind?" real-life concerns cleared Jude's head.

"It's cold outside. Maybe some sweet potato chili?"

"Sounds great. Want some help chopping veg?" Jude smiled at her daughter, her stalwart protector, Rufus, smirking by her side.

Mother and daughter walked down the stairs arm in arm, Rufus running along the steps as close as he could get without getting stepped on.

"That was excellent chili, Abby. Your skill in the kitchen outdoes mine. Feel free to cook as often as possible," Jude smiled contentedly at a beaming Abby.

"Thanks, Mom. Now you can wash up!" she and the cat bounced off to the living room.

Jude cleared the table and put the leftover chili in a container in the fridge. As she began to do up the dishes in the small wash basin not unlike the one from Jude's mother's time, she wondered why Susan had never renovated the kitchen so she could at least have an automatic dishwasher.

After Mom's funeral, I was sure that Susan would start in right away redoing everything she had complained about around the house for years, including having to do the dishes by hand. But, everything looks just as it did when Mom was alive, except older and more worn out. Not kept up, or just the ravages of time in a lived-in space?

Jude kept her mind occupied with such things until she finished the clean-up and walked into the living room where she found Abby asleep on the couch, television blaring, and Rufus curled up close by. Jude turened off the television and roused her daughter enough to steer her up the stairs to her bed and get her tucked in.

Sometimes, she is still such a little girl, Jude thought as she turned off Abby's bedroom light and made her way to her own room back down the hall.

The light was still on over Bill's overstuffed chair so Jude picked up the binder lying in the seat and sat herself down again. Why am I still bothering with this. I don't think it has any secrets to reveal at this point, she thought.

She had started to feel certain that she would never know the true story of Freddie Sanborn's murder. Still, she couldn't help but wonder if Bill's suicide had anything to do with that teenager's death.

"This damnable scrapbook! I should have burned it that first night!" she shrieked as silently as possible so as not to wake Abby.

If Bill's ghost is lurking and listening, she thought defiantly, then he better tell me what the hell he was doing making these notes. Without the notes, I *would* have burned these pages on the first day.

But, Nathan Sanborn's visit and his revelations about his father's suspicions had roused Jude's again. She was determined now to reread everything—newspaper articles in the scrapbook, her own notes to articles in the archives—and to rethink the possible targets of Bill's cryptic notes in those scrapbook pages.

Jude's neck strained from staring down at the scrapbook pages along with her other notes. She sighed again and pushed it all away from her.

I can't make sense of this jumble, maybe I should revisit the transcript of the trial. Even as she thought this, she was dismissing it. I have my own work to do, Abby to take care of, and a big decision to make about what to do with this house come the new year. To bed for now.

About noon, Jude had sent the last proofed chapter back to the publisher and was coming down the stairs thinking about her book when there was a knock at the door. She stopped on the landing, bent down, and peered unnoticed out of the window. Nathan Sanborn stood on the porch, his head moving from side to side.

"What the hell?" Jude hissed as she stood up and went to the door.

"Nathan, I was just going out," she lied. "What can I do for you?" While she spoke, she stepped out onto the porch sans coat and purse, but successfully blocking his ability to come inside.

"Oh—well, sorry to bother you. I'm just leaving town and wanted to say thank you for your, ah, indulgence, in sorting me out," his facial expression was as unconvincing as his tone. He shifted his weight from foot to foot and looked at Jude.

"Of course. Now, I really must grab my things and go. Have a safe trip back to Ohio," she stepped back and closed the two doors.

Jude leaned on the inside of the oak door, took a deep breath, and grabbed her coat and purse from the chair by the phone. She hadn't really planned to go anywhere but thought she should maintain the masquerade as he got into his car and drove away. But, Nathan Sanborn was still standing on the porch when she opened the door to leave her house.

Shutting the two doors quickly behind her, Jude frowned, "Still here? Do you have something more you want to ask, Nathan? I'm really in kind of a hurry."

"I just wanted to know if you ever heard Bill Franklin or your sister say anything about my late uncle's death?"

"No." Jude knew it was abrupt and not what he wanted to hear, but it was, after all, the truth.

Nathan Sanborn stood another moment staring at Jude before he turned to walk down the stairs, throwing a "Thanks" over his shoulder as he walked to his car.

Jude watched him get in and back out of her driveway before she started off the porch toward her own car. When she reached for the door handle, she turned slightly to make sure that he had cleared the stop sign and topped the hill. Then, she pulled her hand back and reversed course until she was back in the house.

She marched into the house and straight up the stairs to her room, grabbed Bill's scrapbook pages and her own notes. She practically tripped over Rufus when she stomped out of her room and down the stairs as the cat had been at his post at the landing window since Nathan Sanborn's first knock.

"Rufus, dammit," she huffed at the cat as she struggled to keep her balance on the last stair. Rufus, naturally offended, rushed back up the stairs, but wisely out of Jude's way.

Jude finally dropped her purse in the entry hall just outside the kitchen but didn't remove her coat. She continued into the kitchen still with scrapbook pages and notes in hand. As she reached in the drawer for matches, she remembered that it was broad daylight, had been dry weather for a week, so she dare not use the burn bin.

But, she remembered, the fireplace in the living room has a fresh batch of logs and kindling waiting for tonight.

Jude dropped to her knees on the hearth as she pulled the scrapbook pages out of the old binder. Then, she laid those pages and her notes on top of her legs as she sat back on her heels.

I can tear all this paper into long strips or stuff it whole under the logs. But, instead of doing either, she just sat there looking from the papers on her lap to the logs on the grate.

"Okay, I'll light the fire first and then stick the pages between the logs one at a time. That should be satisfying," she grimaced as she spoke quietly to the empty room.

Jude lit a match and touched it to the kindling slowly waving it from one end of the kindling pieces to the other until they caught fire. She was still in front of the fireplace sitting on the hearth on her heels when her daughter came home.

"Mom, what are you doing? We usually light a fire after dinner. Were you cold?" Abby came up behind her mother now and touched her shoulder. "Mom?"

The touch of her daughter's hand woke Jude from her reverie, but she kept looking into the fire.

"Uh, yes, cold today," she stammered.

"What's that on your lap, Mom?" Abby reached for the pile of papers and began to scan them, one page after the other. "Mom, what are these old articles taped to each page with weird comments alongside?"

Jude finally stood up and turned to her daughter who was holding the papers and frowning.

"I found a binder. That one over on the chair. The first day I was here. In Bill's den room, the room that connects to mine. The binder had these pages in it."

"But, why would you keep these. They're from decades ago, yeah? Look at this date, June 23, 1968!"

"Yes, that—oh, my god, that's the connection. Bill killed himself on June 23 this year, and his friend was murdered on June 23, 1968. That's what this is all about!"

"Mom? What are you saying? Did Bill murder this kid. What's his name?" Abby rifled through the pages in her hand until she found what she needed. "Freddie Sanborn."

"No. Maybe. No, I can't believe that Bill ever could do that. But, the, oh my god, 50th anniversary of Sanborn's death was the day Bill killed himself. That can't be a coincidence. Can it?"

Abby thought Jude was hyperventilating and made her mother sit down on the couch. "Yoga breathing, Mom. Come on," Abby coached.

Jude took several deep breaths (mostly to please her daughter). "I'm alright, Sweetie. I was actually holding my breath, I think. Let me tell you what I've been doing with this stuff."

Forty-five minutes later, Jude had revealed nearly everything from the moment she found the binder with the scrapbook and notes inside, including showing Abby the picture of the three boys in Bill's yearbook. Jude also gave Abby a summary of the notes she took at the historical archives in town. When she showed her daughter the yearbook picture, she also explained that the third boy in the picture next to Bill and Freddie Sanborn was Jude's own brother, Robbie, the one she never knew and no one ever talked about.

"Wow, I can't believe you didn't tell me all this sooner. I could have helped. Done something," Abby's tone was a bit hurt but mostly excited.

"I'm sorry, baby. If you had been here when I discovered the binder, I probably would have. But by the time you arrived, I had put it away to get my book manuscript to the publisher on schedule and, well, I actually forgot about it until the day I sent that off. You came home from school that afternoon, and we went out to dinner to celebrate, remember? After I sent the book off, I came upon the scrapbook again looking for a tissue in the den cabinets. I can't remember why. Even when I found it again, I used it more as a distraction before the proofs arrived than anything else. But, the next day, I did go downtown after I dropped you off and hit the archives in the local history museum, for a bit. I, uh, that was pretty much all there was to it."

Jude knew she was committing sins of omission but couldn't believe that the whole business with Jim Sherman/Nathan Sanborn would do anything but upset Abby's long-looked-for peace of mind with the house and this town.

"Well, are you going to burn all that?" Abby queried with raised eyebrow.

Her innocent and, Jude had to admit, reasonable question hung in the air between them for a moment before Jude could reply, "Oh, I think I might give this to the local history folks to see if they want it for the file on this case."

Jude didn't convince herself, but Abby seemed satisfied with her answer.

"I'm starving! Can we roast some veggie dogs and marshmallows in the fire?"

Abby's child-like request relieved Jude's tension immediately, and with Rufus complaining about *his* lack of dinner, they laughingly walked to the kitchen to tend the cat's need and to gather the food for their own indoor, winter picnic, something that comforted them both, just in different ways.

As they sat on the floor close to the fire eating their picnic repast, Abby gaily related the latest trials and tribulations of ninth grade. The reflection of the fire in Jude's eyes was perfect.

Epilogue
What really happened to Freddie Sanborn

Bill Franklin, Freddie Sanborn, and Robbie Chandler had been best friends since elementary school. In the last week of June, almost a month after their high school graduation, Robbie was about to return to his Army unit, then, probably, on to Vietnam. The three would be getting together as they had been every Friday night since Robbie had come home on leave after boot camp, but, this time, they were going to make that night especially memorable. Robbie was leaving the next morning so they decided just to stay up all night.

Freddie wouldn't be 18 until July, but Bill and Robbie had already turned 18 during the school year. So, as usual, the older two would be in charge of buying the 3.2 beer for the night. The three boys went out in Robbie's car, since tomorrow, he would be turning it over to his 15-year-old sister for the duration. Freddie and Bill had girlfriends, but they wouldn't be seeing them tonight. Boys Only on Robbie's last night, though they never called it that.

Already shit-faced by midnight on the cheap beer they had procured, Bill pulled out a bottle of Wild Turkey as soon as they downed the last of the beers. Bill's youngish uncle had bought it for the boys as a going away present for Robbie. The other two cheered and reached for the bottle in turn after, of course, letting Robbie have the first drink. They coughed, choked, and laughed as they passed the bottle around and sat sprawled along a sandbar near the river that flowed through the north end of town. All the kids knew the sandbars could be dangerous, especially at night, but the trio had long since discovered the one or two safe places to be secure from drowning and the cops.

The more of the rot gut that Robbie drank, the more maudlin he became about his chances in Vietnam. Freddie, the most emotional of the three, couldn't stand to hear Robbie's fears, which matched his own, and suggested they call it a night, but Bill and Robbie howled in dissent. Robbie said they should do something that they'd never forget. As he said it, he picked up an old baseball bat someone had left on the riverbank. At that moment, Bill was looking up at the bridge that spanned the river to let automobile and foot traffic get across to the north part of the town. His idea for an unforgettable adventure was that they should all jump from the middle of the bridge, together, at the same time.

Robbie shook off his dark mood and, whooping loudly, attempted to heave himself up, but he fell as his legs and feet tangled up beneath him. Bill snorted and pulled Robbie by one arm while turning to offer his hand to Freddie who remained seated on the sandbar, head down. "Come on," said Bill. "Robbie leaves in a couple of hours. We've got to do this. All of us."

Freddie dragged himself up and followed the other two up the hill. When they reached the street, Freddie started challenging Bill's "bad idea." Bill and Robbie both scoffed and jeered at him until he went silent.

The three walked unsteadily crossing the bridge on the walkway, all of them holding onto the concrete railing to steady their uneasy gaits. When they reached the middle, Bill started to climb up onto the railing, but car lights flashed at one end of the bridge. Robbie pulled him down.

"Wait, stupid, until there's no cars. Look around first."

Bill was sufficiently chastened or drunk and stood still. Robbie was leaning heavily on the railing and starting to be sick. Bill and Freddie moved away from him checking both ends of the bridge. No cars. No people coming.

Bill said, "Let's do this together. Robbie will just have to hear about our adventure, our bravery later when he stops puking."

The two hauled themselves up onto the top of the concrete rail which was just wide enough for them to stand and turn toward the water.

Steady they were not, but for the moment both were still until Bill suddenly swayed, knocking into Freddie, and sending him over the side. Freddie didn't land in the water because, unknown to the boys, the water had been released over the dam late that afternoon in readiness for the flood waters coming in from overflowing tributaries to the northwest. Only rocks of various sizes, small pools of river water, and wet sand were left on that side of the bridge.

Bill barely kept himself from following Freddie over the side. He jumped down as quickly as he could and peered into the darkness over the side where Freddie had fallen. He called his name repeatedly. Silence. He ran over and grabbed at Robbie who had finally stopped vomiting.

"Freddie! We have to get Freddie," Bill shouted into Robbie's face pulling his friend back to the hillside to retrace their steps to the sandbar.

They stood on the edge of the sandbar and then inched their way forward, sobering up as they went. Robbie still clutched the baseball bat in his right hand and started using it like a barge pole to navigate the wet sand and rock under their feet. Bill, oblivious to the potential danger to himself, practically ran across the muck and mire toward the dark shape he could just make out from the sandbar.

Freddie was dead. Bruised and bloody. His head smashed by a large, near boulder-sized rock, his arms and legs splayed unnaturally around him.

Robbie and Bill stared down at their friend without moving or speaking for what seemed to them hours but was only a few minutes. Then, they heard someone along the sandbank, singing drunkenly, tonelessly.

They looked at each other and started to run the opposite direction when a man emerged from the darkness nearby. The singing stopped, and the man in front of them swayed one way, then the other before falling onto his back without any attempt to stop himself. He had passed out.

Bill had been holding his breath without realizing it when Robbie said, "Man, I can't get into trouble for this. You and I bought the beer. You said we should jump. You. You didn't push Freddie over the side, but?"

Bill defended himself, "Hell, no! What are you saying? I slipped as we stood on the railing ready to jump. I fell sideways into Freddie and he, he had nothing to hold onto. He fell. Now he's dead. What are *we* going to do?"

Robbie, stared at the ground but could only see the bat in his hand. Always the one to contrive excuses for the parents and good at self-preservation, Robbie started devising a plan.

"We could—that old drunk passed out there. He might have killed Freddie."

"What?" Bill couldn't get his head around what Robbie was saying.

"Yeah, man, like he took this bat and beat Freddie to death for, for the rest of that bottle of rot gut. It's got to be back there along the bar where we were sitting unless he already drank it. Doesn't matter. I'll find it. You take the bat."

Robbie took off, and Bill stood frozen in place with fear, grief, and sheer disbelief at Robbie's intent. At what they were about to do.

Robbie wasn't gone long. He returned bottle in hand. It wasn't empty but nearly so. He went over to the old man passed out a few feet away, poured the rest of the contents onto his shirt, and then put the bottle in one of his hands.

Robbie grabbed the bat and pulled on Bill's arm. "Come with me."

They went back to Freddie's body, and, to Bill's horror, Robbie rolled the business end of the bat in Freddie's blood and wiped the other end clean with his own shirt. Holding the bat with his shirt between it and his hand, Robbie ran back to the unconscious drunk and carefully placed the bat in the old man's remaining free hand.

"We can never, ever tell anyone what really happened here. We can go to the police ourselves and tell them that we ran away as the old drunk went after Freddie. Or we can go home and tell our parents that we got separated from Freddie who went off to take a piss while we climbed up to street level to wait for him. He never came back though we yelled his name for a while. We even went back to where we had been on the sandbar earlier. No Freddie," Robbie was insistent, talking fast.

Bill was not happy with this but didn't know what to do. Robbie was leaving tomorrow and…Freddie was dead.

The lies worked well because the drunk old man had been drifting around town in and out of jail for the last year for being vagrant, drunk and disorderly, resisting arrest, the last giving credence to the lie of his violent act.

The case was made by a young DA with the two boys as the star witnesses telling the story Robbie had fabricated on the spot that night. They were local, high school football heroes so no one ever doubted their word, least of all their parents. Freddie's parents and his younger brother, Danny, must grieve and be satisfied that the old man would hang for his crime.

Robbie shipped out to Vietnam very soon after the trial. He was killed during the final phase of the Tet offensive. His parents were notified of his death in late September. After that, Bill alone had to bear the truth and lies of Freddie Sanborn's death.

About the Author

Julie Chappell proclaims that life in retirement on Lake Keystone in Oklahoma with her poet husband, Hank Jones, is Sweet. In her former life as a professor of medieval and early modern English literature and creative writing, she published six books of scholarship, including the monograph *Perilous Passages: The Book of Margery Kempe, 1534-1934* (Palgrave 2013) and the collection of scholarly essays, *Bad Girls and Transgressive Women in Popular Television, Fiction, and Film* (Palgrave 2017) co-edited with Dr. Mallory Young. She also read her creative works widely in a variety of venues in California, Kansas, Texas, and Oklahoma, among other locations, winning the Grand Slam Poetry Prize in Lawrence, Kansas in 1994. Her poetry and prose have appeared in several anthologies and journals including *Revival: Spoken Word from Lollapalooza 94*; *Agave: A Celebration of Tequila in Story, Song, Poetry, Essay, and Graphic Art*; *Elegant Rage: A Poetic Tribute to Woody Guthrie*; *The Call of the Chupacabra*; *Malpaïs Review*; *Voices de la Luna*; *Concho River Review*; *Stone Renga*; *Speak Your Mind: Woody Guthrie Poets Celebrate Freedom of Speech 2019, Poems of Protest & Resistance*; and *Bull Buffalo and Indian Paintbrush (The Poetry of Oklahoma)*. She has three collections of original poetry – *Faultlines: One Woman's Shifting Boundaries* (Village Books Press, 2013); *Mad Habits of a Life* (Lamar University Literary Press, 2019); and, forthcoming from Turning Plow Press in 2021, *As I Pirouette Away*. *Homecoming and Other Mythic Tales* is her first collection of short fiction.